Allegories of Life

Mrs. J. S. Adams

Contents

ALLEGORIES OF LIFE

BY

Mrs. J. S. Adams

I.
THE BELLS.

In the steeple of an old church was a beautiful chime of bells, which for many years had rung out joyous peals at the touch of the sexton's hand upon the rope.

"I'll make the air full of music to-morrow," said the white-haired man, as he lay down to his slumbers. "To-morrow is Christmas, and the people shall be glad and gay. Ah, yes! right merry will be the chimes I shall ring them." Soon sleep gathered him in a close embrace, and visions of the morrow's joy flitted over his brain.

At midnight some dark clouds swept over the tower, while darker shadows of discontent fell on the peaceful chime.

Hark! what was that? A low, discordant sound was heard among the bells.

"Here we have been ringing for seven long years," murmured the highest bell in the chime.

"Well, what of it? That's what we are placed here for," said a voice from one of the deeper-toned bells.

"But I have rung long enough. Besides, I am weary of always singing one tone," answered the high bell, in a clear, sharp voice.

"Together we make sweetest harmony," returned the bell next the complainer.

"I well know that, but I am tired of my one tone, while you can bear monotony. For my part, I do not mean to answer to the call of the rope to-morrow."

"What! not ring on Christmas Day!" exclaimed all the bells together.

"No, I don't. You may exclaim as much as you please; but, if you had common sympathy, you would see in a moment how weary I am of singing this one high tone."

"But we all have to give our notes," responded a low, sweet-voiced bell.

"That's just what I mean to change. We are all weary of our notes, and need change."

"But we should have to be recast," said the low-toned bell, sadly.

"Most certainly we should. *I* should like the fun of that. Now how many of you will be silent in the morning when the old sexton comes to ring us?"

"I will," answered the lowest-toned bell, boldly.

"If part of us are silent and refuse to ring, of what use will the rest be?" said one who had remained quiet until then. "For a chime all of us are needed," she added, sadly.

"That's just the point," remarked the leader. "If all will be still, none will be blamed: the people will think we are worn out and need making over. So we shall be taken down from this tower where we have been so long, and stand a chance of seeing something of the world. For *my* part, I am tired to death of being up here, and seeing nothing but this quiet valley."

A murmur ran from one to another, till all agreed to be silent on the morrow, though many of the chime would have preferred to ring as usual.

The man who had presented the bells to the church returned at midnight, after a long journey to his native valley, bringing with him a friend, almost solely to hear the beautiful chime on the morrow.

As he passed the church, on his way home, the murmuring of the bells was just ceasing. "The wind moves them--the beautiful bells," he said. "But to-morrow you shall hear how sweet they will sing," he added, casting a loving glance up to the tower where hung the bells.

A few miles from the valley, close to the roadside, stood a cottage inhabited by a man and wife whose only child was fast fading from the world.

"Raise me up a little, mother," said the dying boy, "so I can hear the Christmas chime. It will be the last time I shall hear them here, mother. Is it almost morning?"

The pale mother wiped the death-dew from his brow and kissed him, saying, "Yes, dear, it's almost morning. The bells will chime soon as the first ray comes over the hills."

Patiently the child sat, pillowed in his bed, till the golden arrows of light flashed over the earth. Day had come, but no chime.

"What can be the matter?" said the anxious mother, as she strained her eyes in the direction of the tower.

What if the old sexton were dead? The thought took all her strength away. If death had taken him first, who would lay her boy tenderly away?

"Is it almost time?"

"Almost, Jimmy, darling. Perhaps the old sexton has slept late."

"Will the bells chime in heaven, mother?"

"Yes, dear, I hope so."

"Will they ring them for me if--if--I--mother! hark! the bells *are* ringing! The good old sexton has gone to the church at last!"

The boy's eyes glistened with a strange light. In vain the mother listened. No sound came to *her* ears. All was still as death.

"Oh, how beautiful they sing!" he said, and fell back and died.

Other chimes fell on his ear, sweeter far than the bells of St. Auburn.

For more than an hour the old sexton had been working at the ropes in vain. No sound come forth from either bell.

"What can be the matter?" he exclaimed, nervously. "For seven long years they have not failed to ring out their tones. I'll try once more." And he did so, vigorously.

Just then the figure of a man stood in the doorway. It was the owner of the chime. He had gone to the sexton's house, not hearing the bells at the usual hour, thinking he had overslept; and, not finding him, had sought him at the church.

He tried the ropes himself, but with no more success than the sexton.

"What can it mean?" he said, as he turned sorrowfully away.

It was a sad Christmas in the pleasant valley. To have those sweet sounds missing, and on such a day,--it was a loss to all, and an omen of ill to many.

The next day, workmen were sent to the tower to examine the bells. No defect was perceptible. They were sound and whole, and no mischief-making lad, as some had suggested, had stolen their tongues.

The bells were taken down and carried to a distant city to be recast.

"There! didn't I tell you we should see the world?" said their leader, after they were packed and on their way.

"I don't think we are seeing much of it now, in this dark box," answered one of the bells.

"Wait till we are at our journey's end. We are in a transition state now. Haven't

I listened to the old pastor many a time, and heard him say those very words? I could not comprehend them then, but I can now. Oh, how delightful it is to have the prospect of some change before us!" Thus the old bell chatted to the journey's end, while the other bells had but little to say.

Three days later they were at the end of their long ride, and placed, one by one, in a fiery furnace. Instead of murmurs now, their groans filled the air.

"Oh, for one moment's rest from the heat and the hammer! Oh, that we were all at the sweet vale of St. Auburn!" said the leader of all their sorrow.

"How sweetly would we sing!" echoed all.

"It's a terrible thing to be recast!" sighed the deepest-toned bell; and he quivered with fear as they placed him in the furnace.

At last, after much suffering, they were pronounced perfect, and repacked for their return.

The same tone was given to each, but the quality was finer, softer, and richer than before. The workmen knew not why--none but the suffering bells, and the master hand who put them into the furnace of affliction.

They were all hung once more in the tower--wiser and better bells. Never again was heard a murmur of discontent from either because but one tone was its mission. In the moonlight they talk among themselves, of their sad but needful experience, and of the lesson which it taught them,--as we hope it has our reader,-- that each must be faithful to the quality or tone which the Master has given us, and which is needful to the rich and full harmonies of life.

II.
THE HEIGHT.

There was once an aged man who lived upon an exceeding high mountain for many years; but, as his strength began to decline, he found the ascent so tedious for his feeble steps that he went into the valley to live.

It was very hard for him to give up the view from its lofty height of the sun which sank so peacefully to rest. Long before the sleepers in the valley awoke, he was watching the golden orb as it broke through the mists and flung its beauties over the hills.

"This must be my last day upon the mountain top," he said. "The little strength which is left me I must devote to the culture of fruit and flowers in the valley, and no longer spend it in climbing up and down these hills, whose tops rest their peaks in the fleecy clouds. I have enjoyed many years of repose and grandeur, and must devote the remainder of my life to helping the people in the valley."

At sunset the old man descended, with staff in hand, and went slowly down the mountain side. Such lovely blossoms, pink, golden, and scarlet, met his eye as he gazed on the gardens of the laborers, that he involuntarily exclaimed, "I fear I have spent my days not wisely on yonder mountain top, taking at least a third of my time in climbing up and down. Richer flowers grow here in the valley; the air is softer, and the grass like velvet to the tread. I'll see if there is a vacant cottage for me."

Saying this, he accosted a laborer who was just returning from his toil: "Good man, do you know of any cottage near which I can rent?"

"Why! you are the old man from the mountain," exclaimed the astonished person addressed.

"I am coming to the valley to live. I am now seeking a shelter."

"Yonder," answered the man, "is a cottage just vacated by a man and wife.

Would that suit you?"

"Anything that will shelter me will suit," was the answer. "Dost thou know who owns the house?"

"Von Nellser, the gardener. He lives down by the river now, and works for all the rich men in the valley."

"I'll see him to-night," said the old man, and, thanking his informant, was moving on.

"But, good father, the sun has already set; the night shades appear. Come and share my shelter and bread to-night, and in the morning seek Von Nellser."

The old man gladly accepted his kind offer. "The vale makes men kindly of heart and feeling," he said, as he uncovered his head to enter the home of the laborer. A fair woman of forty came forward, and clasped his hand with a warmth of manner which made him feel more at ease than many words of welcome would have done.

The three sat together at supper, and refreshed themselves with food and thought.

He retired early to the nice apartment assigned him, and lay awake a long time, musing on the past and the present. "Ah, I see," he said to himself, "why I am an object of wonder and something of awe to the people of the valley. I have lived apart from human ties, while they have grown old and ripe together. I must be a riddle to them all--a something which they have invested with an air of veneration, because I was not daily in their midst. Had it been otherwise, I should have been neither new nor fresh to them. How know I but this is God's reserve force wherewith each may become refreshed, and myself an humble instrument sent in the right moment to vivify those who have been thinking alike too much?"

He fell asleep, and awoke just as the sun was throwing its bright rays over his bed. "Dear old day-god," he said, with reverence, and arose and dressed himself, still eying the sun's early rays. "One of thy golden messengers must content me now," he said, a little sadly. "I can no longer see thee in all thy majesty marching up the mountain side; no longer can I follow thee walking over the hill-tops, and resting thy head against the crimson sky at evening: but smile on me, Sun, while in the vale I tarry, and warm my seeds to life while on thy daily march."

The old man went from his room refreshed by sleep, and partook of the bread and honey which the kind woman had ready for him. Then, thanking them for their hospitality, he departed.

The laborer and wife watched him out of sight, and thought they had never seen anything more beautiful than his white hair waving in the morning breeze.

At dusk a light shone in the vacant cottage, and they sent him fresh cakes, milk, and honey for his evening meal.

*   *   *   *   *

Ten years passed away. The old man had cultured his land, and no fairer flowers or sweeter fruits grew in the valley than his own. He had taught the people many truths which he had learned in his solitary life on the mountain, and in return had learned much from them. He faded slowly away. The brilliant flowers within his garden grew suddenly distasteful to him. He longed to look once more on a pure white blossom which grew only at the mountain top. With its whiteness no flower could compare. There were others, growing half way up, that approached its purity, but none equaled the flower on the summit.

"I should like, of all things," answered the old man, when they desired to know what would most please him,--for he had become a great favorite in the valley,--"to look once more upon my pure white flower ere I die; but it's so far to the mountain top, none will care to climb."

"Thou *shalt* see it!" exclaimed a strong youth, who was courageous, but seldom completed anything he undertook, for lack of perseverance.

The old man blessed him. He started for the mountain, and walked a long way up its side, often missing his footing, and at one time seeking aid from a rotten branch, which broke in his grasp and nearly threw him to the base.

After repeated efforts to reach the summit, he found a sweet, pale blossom growing in a mossy nook by a rock.

"Ah! here it is--the same, I dare say, as those on the mountain top. So what need of climbing farther? What a lucky fellow I am to save so many steps for my-self!" and he went down the mountain side as fast as he could, amid the rank and tangled wood, with the flower in his hand.

Day was walking over the meadows with golden feet when he entered the cottage and placed the blossom exultingly in the old man's palm.

"What! so quick returned?" he said. "Thou must have been very swift--but this, my good young man, never grew on the mountain top! Thee must have found this half way up. I remember well those little flowers--they grew by the rocks where I used to rest when on my journey up."

The crowd who had come to see the strange white flower now laughed aloud, which made the youth withdraw, abashed and much humbled. Had he been strong of heart, he would have tried again, and not returned without the blossom from the mountain top. Many others tried, but never had the courage to reach its height; while the old man daily grew weaker.

"He'll die without setting eyes on his flower," said the good woman who had given him shelter the night he came to the valley. She had not the courage to try the ascent, but she endeavored to stimulate others to go to the top and bring the blossom to cheer his heart. She offered, as reward, choice fruits and linen from her stores; but all had some excuse, although they loved the old man tenderly: none felt equal to the effort.

Towards noon, a pale, fragile girl, from a distant part of the vale, appeared, who had heard of his desire, and stood at the door of his cottage and knocked.

"What dost thou wish?" he asked from within.

"To go to the mountain for the flower and place it in thy hand," she answered, as she entered his room and meekly stood before him.

"Thou art very frail of body," he replied, "but strong of heart. Go, try, and my soul will follow and strengthen thee, fair daughter."

She kissed his hand, and departed.

The morning came, and she returned not. The end of the second day drew nigh, and yet she came not back.

"Pooh, pooh!" exclaimed one of a group of wood-cutters near by the cottage. "Such a fool-hardy errand will only be met by death. The old man ought to be content to die without sight of his flower when it costs so much labor to get it."

"So think me," said his comrade, between the puffs of his pipe; "so think me. Our flowers are pretty, and good 'nough, too. Sure, he orter be content with what grows 'round him, and not be sending folk a-climbing." This said, he resumed his smoking vigorously, and looked very wise.

*   *   *   *   *

The aged man of the mountain was passing rapidly away. The kind neighbors laid him for the last time on his cot, and sat tearfully around the room. Some stood in groups outside, looking wistfully towards the mountain; for their kind hearts could not bear to see him depart without the flower to gladden his eyes.

"The girl's gone a long time," remarked one of the women.

"The longer she's gone, the surer the sign she's reached the mountain top. It's a long way up there, and a weary journey back. My feet have trod it often, and I know all the sharp rocks and the tangled branches in the way. But she will come yet. I hear footsteps not far away."

"But too late, we fear, for your eyes to behold the blossom, should she bring it."

"Then put it on my grave--but hark! she comes--some one approaches!"

Through the crowd, holding high the spotless flower, came the fair girl, with torn sandals and weary feet, but with beaming eyes. The old man raised himself in bed, while she knelt to receive his blessing.

"Fair girl,"--he spoke in those clear tones which the dying ever use,--"the whiteness of this blossom is only rivaled by the angels' garments. Its spotless purity enters ever into the soul of him who plucks it, making it white as their robes. To all who persevere to the mountain top and pluck this flower, into all does its purity, its essence, enter and remain forever. For is it not the reward of the toiler, who pauses not till the summit is gained?"

"Oh! good man, the mountain view was so grand, I fain would have lingered to gaze; but, longing to lay the blossom in thy hand, I hastened back."

"Thou shalt behold all the grandeur thy toil has earned thee. Unto those who climb to the mountain summit, who mind not the sharp rocks and loose, rough grass beneath their tread,--unto such shall all the views be given; for they shall some day be lifted in vision, without aid of feet, to grander heights than their weary limbs have reached."

The old man lay back and died.

They buried him, with the flower on his breast, one day just as the sun was setting. Ere the winter snows fell, many of the laborers, both men and women, went up the mountain to its very top, and brought back the white blossoms to deck his grave.

*　　*　　*　　*　　*

The summit only has the view, and the white flower of purity grows upon it. Shall we ascend and gather it? or, like the youth, climb but half the distance, and cheat our eyes and souls of the view from the height?

III.
THE PILGRIM.

One sultry summer day a youthful pilgrim sat by the roadside, weary and dispirited, saying, "I cannot see why I was ordered to tarry beside this hard, unsightly rock, after journeying as many days as I have. Something better should have been given me to rest upon after walking so far. If it were only beside some shady tree, I could wait the appearance of the guide. My lot is hard indeed. I do not see any pilgrim here. Others are probably resting beneath green trees and by running brooks. I will look at my directions once more;" and she drew the paper from her girdle and read slowly these words: "Tarry at the rock, and do not go on till the guide appears to conduct you to your journey's end." She folded and replaced the paper with a sigh, while the murmur still went on: "It's very hard, when beyond I see beautiful green trees, whose long branches would shelter me from the burning sun. How thirsty I am, too! My bread is no longer sweet, for want of water. Oh, that I could search for a spring! I am sure I could find one if permitted to go on my journey. If the rock was not so hard I could pillow my head upon it. Ah me! I have been so often told that the guide had great wisdom, and knew what was good and best for us pilgrims; but this surely looks very dark."

Here weariness overcame the pilgrim, and involuntarily she laid her head upon the rock; when, lo! a sudden spring was touched, and the waters leaped, pure and sparkling, from the hard, unsightly spot. This was the guide's provision for his pilgrim. It was no longer mystical why he had ordered her to tarry there.

When she had drank, and the parched throat was cool and the whole being refreshed, the guide appeared rounding a gentle curve of the road, and bade her follow him through a dense forest which lay between the rock and the journey's end. The steps of the pilgrim now were more firm, for trust was begotten within her, and the light of hope gleamed on her brow--as it will at last upon us all, when the waters have gushed from the bare rocks which lie in the pathways of our lives.

At last we shall learn that our Father, the great Guide, leads us where flow living waters, and that he never forsakes us in time of need.

IV.
FAITH.

"Children," said a faithful father, one day, to his sons and daughters, "I have a journey to take which will keep me many days, perhaps weeks, from you; and as we have no power over conditions,--such as storms, sickness, or any of the so-called accidents of life,--I may be detained long beyond my appointed time of absence. I trust, however, that you will each have confidence in me; and, should illness to myself or others detain me, that you will all trust and wait."

"We will, father!" shouted a chorus of voices, which was music to his ears.

With a fond embrace to each, he left them. Slowly he walked down the winding path which led from his home. He heard the voices of his children on the air long after he entered the highway--voices which he might not hear, perchance, for many months. Sweeter than music to his soul were those sounds floating on the summer air. Over the hill and dale he rode till night came on, and then, before reposing, he lifted his soul to heaven for blessings on his household.

With the sun he arose and pursued his journey. The summer days went down into autumn; the emerald leaves changed their hues for gold and scarlet; ripe fruits hung in ruby and yellow clusters from their strong boughs; while over the rocks, crimson vines were trailing. Slowly the tints of autumn faded. Soon the white frosts lay on the meadows like snow-sheets; the days were shorter and the air more crisp and chill. Around the evening fire the household of the absent parent began to gather. While summer's beauties abounded they had not missed him so much, but now they talked each to the other, and grew strangely restless at his long delay.

"Did he not tell us," said the eldest, "that sickness or accident might delay him?"

"But he sends us no word, no sign, to make us at rest."

"The roads may not be passable," replied the brother, whose faith as yet was not dimmed. "Already the snow has blocked them for miles around us, and we know not what greater obstacles lie beyond. No, let us trust our father," he added, with a depth of feeling which touched them all; and for a few days they rested in the faith that he would come and be again in their midst. But, alas! how short-lived is the trust of the human heart! how limited its vision! It cannot pierce the passing clouds, nor stretch forth its hand in darkness.

Together they sat one evening, in outer and inner darkness,--again in the shadows of distrust.

"He will never return," said one of the group, in sad and sorrowing tones.

"My father will come," lisped the youngest of them all,--the one on whom the others looked as but a babe in thought and feeling.

"I am weary with watching," said another, as she went from the window where she had been looking, for so many days, for the loved form. "Our father has forgotten us all," she moaned, and bowed her head and wept.

There was no one to comfort; for all were sad, knowing that naught but a few crusts remained for their morrow's food--and who would provide for the coming days? Lights and fuel too were wanting, and winter but half gone. Even the faith of the eldest had long since departed, and he too had yielded to distrust.

"My father will come," still whispered the little one, strong in her child-trust, while the others doubted.

"It's because she's so young, and cannot reason like us," they said among themselves.

"Perhaps God can speak to her because she is so simple," said one of the household with whom words were few.

They looked at each other as though a ray of sunlight had flashed through their dwelling. Something akin to hope began to spring in their hearts, but died away as the chilling blasts came moaning around them.

Three days passed, while the storm raged and threatened to bury their home beneath the heavy snows. There was no food now to share between them. The last crumb had been given the child to soften her cries of hunger.

"I can stand this no longer," said the eldest, wrapping his garments around him, and preparing to go forth to find labor and bread for his brothers and sisters. "Ah, that I should ever have lived to see this day!"--he murmured--"the day in which we are deserted and forgotten by our father."

The sound of murmuring within now mingled with the sighing of the winds without. He stepped to the door; but for an instant the fierce blasts drove him back--yet but for an instant. "I will not add cowardice to sorrow," he said to them, in reply to their entreaties not to go in the storm. With one strong effort he faced the chilling sleet, which so blinded him that he could not find the path which led to the highway; yet he went bravely on, till hunger and chill overcame him, and he could no longer see or even feel. He grew strangely dizzy, and would have fallen to the ground, but for a pair of strong arms which at that instant held him fast. He was too much overcome to know who it was that thus enfolded him; but soon a well-known voice rose above the wind and the storm,--he knew that his father's arms were about him, and he feared no more. In the hour of greatest need the father had come. There, in that hour of brave effort, he was spared a long exposure to the wintry blast. A carriage laden with food, fuel, and timely gifts, for each, was already on the road, and would soon deposit its bounties at the door of those whose faith had deserted them.

What a happy household gathered around the father that night! There was no need of lamps to reveal the joy on their faces, and the darkness could not hide the tears which coursed down their cheeks. The little one awoke shouting, in her child-trust, "My father has come! me knew him would!"

And they called her Faith from that hour.

The only alloy in the joy of the others was, as the kind father explained to them the causes of his delay, that they had not trusted him with the faith of the little child; and when he told them of the strange people he had been among, who needed counsel and instruction, and their great need of his ministrations, they sorrowed much that doubt had shadowed for a moment their trust in their father.

Thus do we distrust our Heavenly Parent; and when our needs rise like mountains before us, and all *seems* dark, we cry, "Alas! he has forgotten us!" And yet in our deepest night a light appears, his strong arm uplifts us, and we are taught how holy a thing is Faith.

V.
HOPE.

Darkness had been upon the earth for a long time. It was a period of war and bloodshed, crime and disaster.

The old earth seemed draped in habiliments of mourning; and there was cause for aching hearts, for out of many homes had gone unto battle sons, fathers, and husbands, who would return no more. They fell in service; and kind mothers and wives could not take one farewell look at their still, white faces, but must go about their homes as though life had lost none of its helps.

*   *   *   *   *

"The poor, sad earth!" said one of a glad band, belonging to a starry sphere above. "I long to comfort its people; but my mission is given me to guide souls through the death valley, and bear them to their friends in the summer-land. I must not leave my post of duty. Who will go?"

"I will," said Love, in sweet, silvery tones.

"You are too frail to descend into such darkness as at present envelops the earth; beside, they need another, a different element just now, to prepare the way for better things."

"Who shall it be?" they all said, and looked from one to the other.

"Hope," said their leader, the queen of the starry band.

There was to be high festival that night, in a temple dedicated to the Muses; and it was quite a sacrifice for any of their number to leave their happy sphere, for one so dark as that of earth.

Hope came forward at the mention of her name, holding in her hand the half-finished garland which she had been twining for one of the Graces.

"Wilt thou go to earth to-night, fair Hope?" asked the queen.

The star on her fair brow glittered brighter as she said unhesitatingly, "I will."

"Your mission will be to carry garlands to every habitation which has a light within. The others you cannot, of course, discern. Come now, and let me clasp this strong girdle about thy waist, to which I shall attach a cord, by which to let you down to earth."

They filled her arms with garlands, and flung some about her neck, till she was laden and ready to go.

"Now," said their leader, "descend on this passing cloud; and while you are gone we will sing anthems for you, to keep your heart bright and linked to ours."

Then she fastened the cord to her golden girdle, and let her down gently from the skies.

*   *   *   *   *

In a little cottage by a roadside sat Mary Deane and her sister, reading. They were two fair orphans whose father and brother were lost in battle.

"Let's put out the light, and look at the stars awhile," said the youngest.

"Not yet, dear, it's too early. There may be some passer-by, and a light is such a comfort to a traveler on the road. Many a time our neighbor's light has sent a glow over me which has enabled me to reach home much sooner, if not in better humor."

"As you like, sister,--but hark! I thought I heard footsteps."

They listened, and, hearing nothing more, finished their reading and retired to rest.

On opening their door the next morning, their eyes were gladdened by a lovely garland which hung on the knob. The flowers were rich in, perfume and color--unlike anything they had seen on earth.

Much they marveled, and wondered from whence they came, and still greater was their joy to find they did not fade.

Hope found a great many dwellings with lights in them, but had to pass many, as there was no lamp to signal them. At the door of the former she left garlands to gladden the inmates.

"It's no use to waste our oil: we have nothing to read or interest us," said one of two lonely women, on the night Hope came to the earth. So they sat down gloomily together, the darkness adding to their cheerlessness, while a bright glow within would have gladdened them and all without.

Hope went by, laden with garlands, just as they took their seats in the shadows. She would gladly have left them, for she had enough and to spare; but, seeing no sign of a habitation, walked on.

The two women talked of the dreary world until they went to rest. What was their surprise, in the morning, to find their neighbors rejoicing over their mysterious gifts.

"Why had we none?" they said again and again. "The poor never have half as much given them as the wealthy," they cried, and went back to their gloom and despair.

"Did you find a wreath on your doorstep this morning?" inquired a bright, hopeful woman at noon, who had brought them a part of her dinner.

"No, indeed!" they answered. "Did you find one on yours?"

"The handsomest wreath I ever saw. Who ever could have made one so lovely? But"--she stopped suddenly, on seeing their sad faces. "You shall have part of mine: I will cut it in two."

"Never!" said the eldest quickly. "There is some reason why we were omitted; and, until we can know the cause, you must keep your wreath unbroken."

It was very noble of her to come out of herself and refuse to accept what she instinctively felt did not belong to her.

A week passed away. A child in the village had had strange dreams concerning the gifts, which, in substance, was that a beautiful angel had come from the stars above, and brought flowers to every house in which a light was seen.

"We did not have any light that night,--don't you remember?" remarked the eldest of the women, as their neighbor told them of the strange dream.

"There must be *something* in it," answered the little bright-eyed woman. "For all the dwellings had flowers which were lighted."

"I suppose we ought always to be more hopeful," said the women together. "The lamps of our houses should typify the light of hope, which should never be dim, nor cease burning."

*   *   *   *   *

Hope was taken up, by a golden cord, to her abode. The starry group sang heavenly anthems to refresh her, and Love twined a fresh garland for her brow. They held another festival in the temple, in honor of her and her safe return from the earth.

Ever since she has been the brightest light in the group; and at night, when the clouds rising from the earth obscure all the others, the star on the brow of Hope is shining with a heavenly lustre, and seen by all whose gaze is upward.

VI.
JOY AND SORROW.

Many years ago, two visitors were sent from realms above, to enter the homes of earth's inhabitants, and see how much of true happiness and real sorrow there were in their midst. Hand in hand they walked together, till they entered a pleasant valley nestled among green hills. At the base of one of these stood a cottage covered with roses and honeysuckles, which looked very inviting; and the external did not belie the interior.

The family consisted of a man and wife somewhat advanced in years, an aged and infirm brother, and two lovely young girls, grandchildren of the couple.

The pleasant murmur of voices floated on the air,--pleasant to the ear as the perfume of the roses climbing over the door was to the sense of smell. It chimed with the spell of the summer morning, and the sisters knew that harmony was within.

"Let us enter," said Joy.

Sorrow, who was unwilling to go into any abode, lingered outside.

Within, all was as clean and orderly as one could desire: the young girls were diligently sewing, while before them lay an open volume, from which they occasionally read a page or so, thus mingling instruction with labor.

Joy entered, and accosted them with, "A bright morning."

"Very lovely," answered the girls, and they arose and placed a chair for their visitor.

"We have much to be grateful for every day, but very much on such a day as this," remarked the grandmother.

"You're a busy family," said Joy.

"Yes, we all labor, and are fond of it," answered the woman, looking fondly at the girls. "We have many blessings, far more than we can be grateful for, I sometimes think."

"Yes, I tell mother," broke in the husband, "that we must never lose sight of our blessings; in fact, they are all such, though often in disguise."

At that moment Sorrow looked in at the open door. It was so seldom that *she* was recognized that she longed to enter.

"You have a friend out there: ask her in," said the woman.

Joy turned and motioned her sister to enter. She came in softly, and sat beside Joy, while the woman spoke of her family, at the desire of each of the sisters to know of her causes of happiness.

"Yes, they are all blessings in disguise," she said, "though I could not think thus when I laid my fair-eyed boy in the grave; nor, later, when my next child was born blind."

"Had you none other?" asked Joy.

"One other, and she died of a broken heart."

Sorrow sighed deeply, and would rather have heard no more; but Joy wished to hear the whole, and asked the woman to go on.

"Yes, she died heart-broken; and these two girls are hers. It was very hard that day to see the hand of God in the cloud when they brought the body of her husband home all mangled, and so torn that not a feature could be recognized; and then to see poor Mary, his wife, pine day by day until we laid her beside him."

"But the blessing was in it, mother: we have found it so. They have only gone to prepare the way, and we have much left us."

The words of the old man were true, and it was beautiful to see the face of his wife as it glowed with recognition.

At that moment the sisters threw back their veils. Such a radiant face was never seen in that cottage as the beaming countenance of Joy; while that of her sister was dark and sad to look upon.

"Oh, stay with us," exclaimed the girls to Joy, as the sisters rose to depart.

"Most gladly would I, but I have a work to perform in your village; and, beside, I cannot leave my sister."

"But she is so dark and sad, why not leave her to go alone?" said the youngest girl, who had never seen Sorrow nor heard of her mission to earth before.

Sorrow was standing in the door and heard her remark. She hoped the day would never come when *she* should have to carry woe to her young heart; but her life was so uncertain she knew not who would be the next whom she would have to envelop in clouds. She sighed, plucked a rose, and pressed it to her nostrils, as though it was the last sweetness she would ever inhale.

"How I pity her!" said the grandmother, her warm, blue eyes filling with tears, as she looked at the bowed form in the doorway.

"Ah, good woman, she needs it; for few recognize her mission to them. She is sent by our master to administer woes which contain heavenly truths, while I convey glad tidings. I shall never leave my sister save when our labors are divided."

Thus spoke Joy, while tears filled the eyes of all.

Then the kind woman went and plucked some roses and gave them to Sorrow, who was weeping.

"I did not half know myself," she said, addressing the sad form; "I thought I could see God's angels everywhere, but this time how have I failed! Forgive me," she said to Sorrow, "and when you are weary and need rest, come to our cottage."

Sorrow gave her a sad but heavenly smile, and the sisters departed to the next abode.

"Did you ever see them before?" asked the children of their grandparents after the sisters had gone.

"Often: they have been going round the world for ages," answered their grandparents.

"But Joy looks so young, grandpa."

"That's because she has naught to do with trouble. She belongs to the bright side. She carries good tidings and pleasure to all; while Sorrow, her sister, administers the woes."

"But Joy is good not to leave her sister."

"She cannot," said the grandparent.

"Cannot! Why?"

"Because Providence has so ordered it that Joy and Sorrow go hand in hand,--pleasure and pain. No two forces in nature which are alike are coupled. Day and night, sunshine and shadow, pleasure and pain, forever."

"But I should like to have Joy stay with us," said Helen, the youngest, to her grandparent.

"We shall ever be glad to see her; but we must never treat her sister coldly or with indifference, as though she had no right to be among us; because, though in the external she is unlovely, within she is equally radiant with her sister,--not the same charm of brilliancy, but a softer, diviner radiance shines about her soul."

"Why, grandpa, you make me almost love her," said Marion, the eldest, while Helen looked thoughtful and earnest.

The seeds of truth were dropped which at some future time would bear fruit.

*   *   *   *   *

It was a large and elegant house at which the sisters stopped next. A beautiful lawn, hedged by hawthorne, sloped to the finely-graded street; while over its surface beds of brilliant flowers were blooming, contrasting finely with the bright green carpet. They ascended the granite steps which led to the portico, and rang the bell. A servant answered the summons, and impatiently awaited their message.

"We would see the mistress of the mansion," said Joy.

They were shown into an elegant drawing-room, so large they could scarcely see the farther end. It was furnished in a most dazzling style, and gave none of that feeling of repose which is so desirable in a home. After what seemed a long time, the lady of the mansion appeared, looking very much as though her visitors were intruders.

"A lovely day," said Joy.

"Beautiful for youth and health," she answered curtly; "but all days are the same to me."

"You are ill, then," said Joy, sympathetically.

"Ill, and weary of this life. Nothing goes well in this world: there is too much sorrow to enjoy anything. But," she added after a brief silence, "you are young, and cannot enter into my griefs."

"I have come for the purpose of bringing you comfort and hope if you will but accept it," answered Joy, modestly.

"A stranger could scarcely show me what I cannot find. Be assured, young maiden, if I had the pleasures you suppose I possess, I should not be tardy in seeing them. No, no: my life is a succession of cares and burdens."

Joy was silent a moment, and then said, "But you have health, a home, and plenty to dispense to the needy, which must be a comfort, at least, in a world of so much need."

"My home is large and elegant, I admit; but, believe me, the care of the servants is a burden too great for human flesh."

Joy thought how much better a cottage was, with just enough to meet the wants of life, than a mansion full of hirelings; and she said, hopefully, "Our blessings ever outnumber our woes. If we but look for them, we shall be surprised each day to see how many they are. I am on a visit to earth," continued Joy, "to see how much real happiness I can find, and help, if possible, to remove obstacles that hinder its advancement. This is my sister, Sorrow," she continued, turning to her, "who, like myself, has a mission, though by no means a pleasant one."

The sisters unveiled their faces.

A flush of pleasure stole over the sallow face of the woman as she gazed upon the brightness of Joy's countenance; but the look quickly faded at the sight of Sorrow's worn and weary features.

"My sister must tarry here," said Joy, as she rose to leave.

"Here! With me? Why! I can scarcely live now. What can I do with her added to my troubles?"

"It is thus decreed," answered Joy. "You need the discipline which she will bring to you."

And she departed, leaving her sister in the elegant but cheerless mansion.

The mistress of the luxurious home had one fair daughter, whom she was bringing up to lead a listless, indolent, and selfish life,--a life which would result in no good to herself or others.

Sorrow grew sadder each day as she saw the girl walking amid all the beauties with which she was surrounded, careless of her own culture. She felt, also, that she must at some time, and it might be soon, be removed from her luxuries, or they from her. Each hour the fair girl's step grew heavier, till at last she was too weak to walk, or even rise from her bed.

"All this comes of having that sad woman here," exclaimed the weeping mother as she bent over her daughter. "I'll have her sent from the house this day." And she rang for a servant to send Sorrow away.

After delivering her message to her maid, she felt somewhat relieved.

The servant went in search of Sorrow, but could not find her either in the house, garden, on the lawn, or among the dark pines where she often walked.

Whither had she fled?

All the servants of the house were summoned to the search; but Sorrow was not to be found, and they reported to the mistress their failure to find her.

"No matter," she replied, "so long as she is no longer among us. Go to your labors now, keep the house very quiet, and be sure, before dark, to lock all the doors, that she may not enter unperceived."

They need not have bolted nor barred her out; for her work was done, and she had no cause to return.

She was sent to the house of wealth to carry the blight of death. Her mission was over, and she was on her way, seeking Joy.

The young girl faded slowly and died.

The mother mourned without hope, and was soon laid beside her daughter. The home passed into the hands of those who felt that none must live for themselves alone; that sorrows must be borne without murmur; and joys appreciated so well that the angel of sorrow may not have to bear some treasure away to uplift the heart and give the vision a higher range.

Sorrow met Joy on the road that night. There was no moon, even the stars were dim; but for the shining face of her sister, she would have passed her. They joined hands, and walked together till morning broke. They came in sight of a low cottage just as the day dawned.

"Oh, dear!" said Sorrow, as they approached the familiar spot, "how often have I been there to carry woe! Do you go now, Joy, and give them gladness!"

"If it is the master's hour I will most gladly," said Joy, looking tenderly on the weary face of her sister, who sat by the roadside to rest awhile while she lifted her heart to heaven, asking that she might no more carry woe to that humble home; and her prayer was answered.

"I feel to go there," said Joy, as Sorrow wiped her tears away. "Wait here till I return;" and she ran merrily on.

She entered the humble home with gladness in her beaming eyes, and, as she bore no resemblance to her sister, they welcomed her with much greeting; nor did they know but for Sorrow, Joy would not have been among them. She talked with them a long time, and listened patiently to the story of their woes.

Sickness, death, and adversity had been their part for many years.

"But they are passing away," said Joy, confidently, "and health and prosperity shall yet be among you."

"We shall know their full value," whispered a voice from the corner of the room which Joy's eyes had not penetrated. On a low cot lay an invalid, helpless and blind.

The tears fell from her own eyes an instant, and then sparkled with a greater brilliancy than before, as she said, "And this, too, shall pass away."

The closed eyes, from which all light had been shut out for seven long years, now slowly opened; the palsied limbs relaxed; life leaped through the veins once more; and she arose from her bed, while the household gathered round her.

A son, who was supposed to have been lost at sea, after an absence of many years returned at that moment, laden with gold and other treasures far greater, than the glittering ore,--lessons of life, which, through suffering, he had wrought into his mind.

Joy departed, amid their tumult of rejoicing, and joined her sister.

The happy family did not miss her for a time; yet when their great and sudden happiness subsided into realization they sought her, but in vain.

They needed her not; for the essence of her life was with them, while she was walking over the earth, carrying pleasure and happiness to thousands; yet doing the work of her father no more than her worn and sad-eyed sister.

VII.
UPWARD.

There was once an aged man who owned and lived in a large house the height of which was three stories. His only child was a daughter, of whom he was very fond, and who listened generally to his words of counsel and instruction; but no amount of persuasion could induce her to ascend to the highest story of their dwelling, where her father spent many hours in watching the varied landscape which it overlooked. It was an alloyed pleasure as he sat there evening after evening alone, looking at the lovely cloud tints, and rivers winding like veins of silver through the meadows. It detracted from his joy to know that the view from the lower window offered naught but trees thickly set and dry hedges.

"Come up, child," he called, morning and evening, year after year, with the same result. It seemed of no avail. "She will die and never know what beauties lie around her dwelling," he said, as he sat looking at the wealth of beauty. It seemed to him that the clouds were never so brilliant, nor the trees and meadows so strangely gilded by the sun's rays, as on that evening. He longed more than ever to share with his child the pleasure he experienced, and resolved upon a plan by which he hoped to attain his wish.

"I will have workmen shut out the light of all the stories below with thick boards, and bar the door that she may not escape. I will give her a harmless drink to-night that will deepen her slumbers while the work is being done; for by these seemingly harsh means alone can I induce my child to ascend."

That night, while she slumbered, the work was done, and she awoke not at the sound of the hammer on the nails. When all was completed, the father ascended to await the rays of morning, and listen for the voice of his child, which soon broke in suppliant tones upon his ears:--

"Father! my father! It's dark! I cannot see!"

"Come up, my child!" still he cried. "Come to me, and behold new glories."

She gave no answer; but he heard her weeping, and groped his way below to lead her up. She no longer resisted. Her steps, though slow, were willing ones: they were upward now, and the father cared not how slow, so long as they were ascending.

Many times she wished to go back, but he urged her on with gentle words and a strong, sustaining arm, till the last landing was reached, and the light, now streaming through the open windows, made words no longer needful. With a bound she sprang to the open casement, exclaiming, "Father, dear father!" and fell, weeping, on his breast.

His wish was granted; his effort was over, and his child could now behold the beauties which had so long thrilled his own soul.

Thus does our Heavenly Father call us upward; and when he sees that we will not leave the common view for grander scenes, and will not listen to his voice, however beseeching, he makes all dark and drear below, that we may be led to ascend higher, where the day-beams are longer, the view more extended, and the air more rarified and pure.

VIII.
THE OAK.

An old and experienced gardener had been watching a tree for many days, whose branches and foliage did not seem to repay him for his care. "I see," he said, a little sadly; "the roots are not striking deep enough: they must have a firmer hold in the earth, and only the wind and the fierce blast will do it."

It was now sunset, and the faithful gardener put away his tools, closed the garden gates, and went into his cottage. Soon a mass of dark clouds began to gather on the horizon. "I am sorry to use such harsh means," he said, waving his hand in the direction of the wind clouds; "but the tree needs to be more firmly rooted, and naught but a violent wind will aid it."

A low, moaning sound went through the air, shaking every bush and tree to its foundation.

"Oh, dear!" sighed the tree. "Oh, the cruel gardener, to send this wind! It will surely uproot me!"

The tree readied forth its branches like arms for help, and implored the gardener to come and save it from the fearful blasts. The flowers at its feet bowed their heads, while the winds wafted their fragrance over the struggling, tempest-tost tree.

"They do not moan, as I do. They cannot be suffering as I am," said the tree, catching its breath at every word.

"They do not need the tempest. The rain and the dew are all they want," said a vine, which had been running many years over an old dead oak, once the pride of the garden. "I heard the gardener say this very afternoon," continued the vine, "that you must be rooted more firmly; and he has sent this wind for that purpose."

"I wonder if *I* am the only thing in this garden that needs shaking," spoke the oak, somewhat indignantly. "There's a poor willow over by the pond that is always weeping and--"

"But," interrupted the vine, "that's what keeps the beautiful sheet of water full to the brim, and always so sparkling,--the constant dropping of her tears; and we ought to render her gratitude. Besides, she is so graceful--"

"Oh, yes: all the trees are lovely but me. I heard the gardener's praise, the other day, of the elms and the maples, and even the pines; but not one word did he say about the oaks. I didn't care for myself in particular, but for my family, which has always been looked up to. Well, I shall die, like my brother, and soon we shall all pass away; but, unlike my brother oak, no one will cling to me as you do, vine, to his old body."

"You're mistaken, sir. The gardener said, but a few days ago, that he should plant a vine just like myself at your trunk if your foliage was not better, so that you might present a finer appearance by the mingling of the vine's soft leaves, and be more ornamental to the garden."

"I'll save him that trouble if my life is spared. I have no desire to be decked in borrowed leaves. The oaks have always kept up a good appearance; but oh, dear me, vine, didn't that blast take your breath away? I fear I *shall* die; but, if I do live, I'll show the gardener what I can do. But, vine," and the voice of the oak trembled, "tell the gardener, when he comes in the morning, if--if I am dead--that--that the dreadful tempest killed instead of helped me."

The wind made such a roaring sound that the oak could not hear her reply, and he tried now to become reconciled to death. He thought much in that brief space of time and resolved, if his life was spared him, that he would try and put forth his protecting branches over the beds of flowers at his feet, to protect them from the blazing sun, and try to be more kind and friendly to all. Deeper and deeper struck the roots into the earth, till a new life-thrill shot through its veins. Was it death?

The oak raised its head. The clouds were drifting to the south. All was calm, and the stars shone like friendly eyes in the heavens above him.

"That oak would have surely died but for the tempest which passed over us," said the gardener, a few weeks later, as he was showing his garden to a friend.

The gardener stood beneath the branches, and saw with pleasure new leaves coming forth and the texture of the old ones already finer and softer.

"It only needed a firmer hold on the earth. The poor thing could not draw moisture enough from the ground before the storm shook its roots and embedded them deeper. If I had known the philosophy of storms before, I need not have lost the other oak."

Here the old gardener sat beneath the branches of the oak, and they seemed to rise and fall as if bestowing blessings on his head. That spot became his favorite resting-place amid his labors for many years. The oak lived to a good old age, and was the gardener's pride. Maidens gathered its leaves and wove garlands for their lovers. Children sported under its boughs. It was blessed and happy in making others so. It had learned the lesson of the storm, and was often heard to say to the young oaks growing up about it, "Sunshine and balmy breezes have their part in our growth, but they are not all that is needful for our true development."

IX.
TRUTH AND ERROR.

A mid the starry realms there lived an old philosopher, a man deep in wisdom, who had two daughters, named Truth and Error, whom he sent to earth to perform a mission to its people; and though he knew that their labors must be united, he could not explain to them why two so dissimilar should have to roam so many years on earth together. Well he knew that, though Truth would in the end be accepted by the people, she must suffer greatly. His life experience had taught him that she must go often unhonored and unloved, while Error, her sister, would receive smiles, gifts, and welcome from the majority. It was a sacrifice to part with his much-loved daughter Truth, and a great grief to be obliged to send Error with her. He placed them, with words of cheer and counsel, in the care of Hyperion, the father of the Sun, Moon, and Dawn, who accompanied them in his golden chariot to the clouds, where he left the two in charge of Zephyr, who wafted them from their fleecy couch to the earth.

One bleak, chilly day, the two were walking over a dreary road dotted here and there with dwellings. The most casual observer might have seen their striking dissimilarity, both in dress and manners. Truth was clad in garments of the plainest material and finish, while Error was decked in costly robes and jewels. The step of the former was firm and slow, while that of the latter was rapid and nervous. The bleak winds penetrated their forms as they turned a sharp angle in the road, when there was revealed to them, on an eminence, a costly and elegant building.

"I shall certainly go in there for the night, and escape these biting blasts," said Error to her sister.

"Although, the house is large and grand," answered Truth, "it does not look as though its inmates were hospitable. I prefer trying my luck in yonder cottage on the slope of that hill."

"And perhaps have your walk for naught," answered Error, who bade a hasty good-by to her sister and entered the enclosure, which must have been beautiful in summer with its smooth lawns, fine trees and beds and flowers. She gave the bell a sharp ring, and was summoned into an elegant drawing-room full of gaily dressed people. Error was neither timid nor bashful, and she accepted the offered courtesies of the family as one would a right. She seated herself and explained to them the object of her call, dwelling largely on the grandeur of her elegant home amid the stars, and tenderly and feelingly upon her relationship with the gods and goddesses, and the numerous feasts which she had attended, so that at her conclusion her hostess felt that herself and family were receiving rather than bestowing a favor.

The evening was spent amid games and pastimes till the hour for retiring, when they conducted her to a warm and elegantly furnished room, so comfortable that it made her long, for a moment, for her sister to share it with her; for, despite the difference in their natures, Error loved her sister. The soft couch, however, soon lulled her to sleep. She, slumbered deeply, and dreamed that Truth was walking all night, cold and hungry, when suddenly a lovely form came out of the clouds. It was none other than Astrea, whom she had seen often in her starry home, talking with Truth. She saw her fold a soft, delicate garment about the cold form of her sister, at the same time saying, in reproving tones, to herself, "This is not the only time you have left your sister alone in the cold and cared for yourself. The sin of selfishness is great, and the gods will succor the innocent and punish the offender."

She closed, and was rising, with Truth in her arms, to the skies, when Error gave such a loud shriek that Astrea dropped her, and a strong current of air took the goddess out of sight. It was well for the earth, which might have been forever in darkness, that Truth was dropped, though hard for her.

Error awoke from her dream, which seemed more real than her elegant surroundings, and resolved to go in search of Truth when the morning came; but a blinding storm of snow and sleet, and the remonstrance of the family, added to her own innate love of ease, left Truth uncared for by one whose duty it was to seek her.

The days glided into weeks, and yet Error remained, much to the wonder of the poorer neighbors around, that Mrs. Highbred should encourage and keep such a companion for her daughters. They could see at a glance that Error was superficial, that she possessed no depth of thought or feeling; and their wonder grew to deep surprise when they saw all the gentry for miles around giving parties in honor of her. Everywhere she was flattered and adored, until she became, if possible, more vain and full of her own conceit.

"You should see the feasts of the gods in our starry realms," she would say, as each one vied with a preceding festivity to outshine its splendor.

After Error left her sister, Truth walked slowly and thoughtfully towards the cottage on the hill-side. She went slowly up the path, which wound in summer by beds of roses, to the door, and rapped gently. It was opened by a fair and beautiful woman, who bade her "walk in" in tones which matched the kindness of her features. The next moment Truth felt her gentle hands removing her hood and cloak, and felt that she was welcome. A table covered with a snowy cloth stood in the centre of the room, on which was an abundant supply of plain, substantial food, more attractive to a hungry traveler than more costly viands. A chair was placed for her by the bright fire, while the air of welcome entered her soul and drew tears from her deep, sad eyes. It was so seldom she was thus entertained--so often that the manner of both high and low made the highway pleasanter than their habitations. How often had she walked alone all night unsheltered, while Error, her sister, reposed on beds of down! The sharp contrast of their lives was the great mystery yet unrevealed. It cost her many hours of deep and earnest thought.

It was so rare that any one gave her welcome that her gratitude took the form of silence. For an instant the kind woman thought her lacking; but when her grateful look upturned to hers, as she bade her sit at the table and partake of the bounties, all doubt of her gratitude departed.

Truth slept soundly all night, and arose much refreshed by her slumbers. The storm of the day would not have detained her from continuing her journey; but the warm and truthful appeal of the woman, who felt the need of such a soul as Truth possessed with whom to exchange thoughts, induced her to remain that day, and many others, which slipped away so happily, and revealed to her that *rest* as well as action is needful and right for every worker.

Truth became a great favorite among the poorer classes of the neighborhood, as she always was whenever they would receive and listen to her words; and it was not long before people of thought, rank, and culture began to notice her and court her acquaintance.

Mrs. Highbred, hearing of her popularity, concluded to give a party and invite her.

Error had never spoken of the relationship between them until the day the invitations were sent. Then, knowing she could no longer conceal the past, she availed herself of the first opportunity to communicate the same to her hostess. Great was the surprise of Mrs. Highbred and her household to learn that the quiet stranger at the cottage was the sister of Error.

"My sister is very peculiar, and wholly unlike myself," remarked Error to her hostess; "and I fear you will find her quite undemonstrative. Although it is my parent's wish that I should be with her, you cannot imagine what a relief it has been to a nature like mine to mingle with those more congenial to my tastes, even for a brief period."

"It must be," answered Mrs. Highbred sympathizingly, and Error congratulated herself on having become installed in the good graces of so wealthy a person.

"Now," she said to herself, "I need not go plodding about the world any longer. Truth can if she likes to; and, as she feels that she has such a mission to perform to the earth, she of course will not remain in any locality long. But, thanks to the gods, who, I think, favor me always, I shall not be obliged to roam any longer. Truth never did appreciate wealth or the value of fine surroundings. She's cast in a rougher mold than I--"

"Ma sends you this set of garnets, and begs you will do her the favor to wear them on the night of the party," said the bearer of a case of jewels, as she laid them on the table, and bounded out of the room before Error could reply. Indeed, her surprise was too great for words had the child remained. "I wonder what Truth will say when she sees them," thought Error, as she glanced again and again at the sparkling gems.

Nothing could be more striking than the contrast between Truth and her sister, both in costume and manner, as they stood apart from the company a moment to exchange a few words.

Error was decked in a costly robe of satin of a lavender hue, to contrast with her gems; while Truth was arrayed in white, with a wreath of ivy on her brow, and the golden girdle around her waist which her father gave her at parting. She wore no gems save an arrow of pearl which Astrea gave her when they parted at the gate of clouds, kept by the goddesses named the Seasons, which opened to permit the passage of the celestials to earth and to receive them on their return.

The simple dress and manners of Truth won the admiration of a few, while the majority paid tribute to Error, who kept her admirers listening to her wonderful adventures amid the region of the stars. Truth spoke but seldom; but what she uttered was food for thought, instead of a constellation of merely dazzling words.

A careful observer might have seen that the elder members lingered, attracted by her simple charms, near Truth, as did also the youngest portion of the company, while youth and middle age could not divine her sphere of pure and earnest thought. The few who sought her would gladly have continued the acquaintance, and they invited her to their dwellings; but on the morrow she would set forth on her journey, feeling that she had implanted in the minds of a few the love of something beyond externals and mere materialisms.

Her earthly mission was to traverse hill and plain throughout the land, and sow seeds of righteousness which would spring up in blossoms of pearl long after her weary feet had traversed other lands and sown again in the rough places the finer seeds.

At early dawn Truth went forth from the cottage and the kind woman who had sheltered her. They had enjoyed much together in their mutual relation. Trust met trust, hope clasped hope, and each was stronger for the soul exchange.

When the sun rose in the heavens Truth was on her way, while Error, tossed in feverish dreams upon her bed, thought the Sun was angry with her, and was sending his fierce rays upon her head to censure or madden her. But he was only trying to waken her and urge her to go on with her sister. A sense of relief came when she opened her eyes and found it was, after all, only a dream. Yet the pleasure was brief; for a sharp pain shot through her temples, her brow was feverish, and her pulses throbbed wildly. "Oh, for the pure air and the cool, refreshing grass!" she cried. "Oh, better the highway with its friendly blossoms than this couch of down and this stifled atmosphere which I am breathing!" How she longed for Truth then, to cool her brow with the touch of her gentle hand. "Come back, oh, come to me, Truth!" she cried, so hard that the whole household heard and came to her bedside.

"She is ill and delirious!" they cried in one voice. The family physician was summoned, who pronounced the case fearful and her life fast ebbing.

"For whom shall we send?" said Mrs. Highbred, who was unused to scenes of distress and now longed to have her guest far from her dwelling.

"For her sister Truth," said one.

"Truth--Truth," said the physician. "Is it possible?" and he gazed from one to another for revelation.

"Truth is her sister," said one of the younger members, and added, "I think she is far better and prettier than Error,--"

"Far better, far better," continued the physician, looking only at the child, and inwardly saying, "Out of the mouths of babes and sucklings come words of wisdom."

"I met her on the hill,--the one you call Truth," he said, in answer to the searching look of Mrs. Highbred, who by manner and inquiry plainly manifested her desire to have an end of the unusual state of things.

"I will go for her. She will return with me," continued the doctor, "and soon we will find some spot to which we can remove Error."

A look of relief came over the face of the lady as he departed.

Truth heard not the sound of the horses, nor the rumbling of wheels as they approached, so intent were her thoughts on separation from her sister and her own strange mission to earth; and she scarce sensed whither she was going, when the kind man courteously lifted her into his carriage. But when she stood by the fevered, unconscious form of Error, a few moments later, all her clearness of thought was at her command.

"Carry her to the cottage on the hill-side," she said, as she bound a cool bandage on her sister's brow.

They bore her there, and, as though in mercy, a dark cloud shut off the sun's rays, and their fierce glare was obscured during transit from the home of splendor to the humble cottage.

There for many weeks Truth nursed her sister, while the kind hostess and kind neighbors aided by words and deeds through the long night watches.

Error arose from her illness somewhat wiser, and firmly fixed in her determination to follow Truth and share her fate to their journey's end.

Thus, reader, shall we ever find them together while we dwell on earth, and perchance in the regions above. Let us trust that they are wisely related; and, while we love, reverence, and admire the purity of Truth, let us seek also courteously to endure Error as an opposing force, which, though it may seem for a time to work our discomfort and hinder us in our progress, yet gives us strength, as the rower on the stream is made stronger by the counter currents and eddies with which he has to contend.

X.
THE TREE.

A large shade-tree grew near a house, and under its branches the children played every summer day. It seemed to take great delight in their voices, and shook its green boughs over their heads, as though it would join in their sports and laughter. But, alas! one day it got a foolish idea into its head--it grew discontented, and felt that its sphere of usefulness was too limited.

At that moment dark clouds gathered, a fearful tempest arose, and a strong current of wind, soon set the giant tree swinging with such violence that it was torn from the earth and lay like a broken column on the ground.

"Now I shall be something: I've got my roots out of the old earth. Bah! such a heap of old black loam, to be sure, as I have been in! I'll soon shake it off, however, and then the world will see that *I* can soar as well as other things."

There was a terrible quaking and noise as the old tree tried to rise from its recumbent position. The sun's rays were fast parching its roots, causing sharp pains to shoot through its branches.

"Oh, dear!" said the tree. "I hope I shall be able to get on my feet soon, else people will be laughing at me for lying here so helpless."

The golden sun went down behind the hills. Its rays could not gild the top of its branches now, and the tree missed the benediction of its parting rays. A feeling akin to homesickness came over it, and a longing, as the dews of evening came, to be once more rooted to the earth.

A wild wind sang a dirge all through the night, and ceased not till day darted over the hills. It was not very pleasant for the old tree to hear the children's regrets and words of grief as they came around it in the morning to play and sit as usual under its pleasant shade. It had hoped to have been far away by dawn, and thus have escaped the sound of their voices.

"I'll wait till they are gone, and then I must be off," said the tree softly.

"Papa will cut it all up into wood, I know," said the youngest of the group, a bright, three-year-old boy.

"I am going to have a piece of one of the boughs to make a cane of," said another.

"And oh, dear me!" sighed little blue-eyed May. "I can't have any more autumn leaves to make pretty wreaths of for mamma."

Poor old tree! how it had mistaken its mission and its relation to the earth! So it is with people who lament the position in which Providence has placed them. In vain the old tree tried to rise: its branches withered, its leaves dropped one by one away, and rustled on the lawn. It found, to its sorrow, that it was not made for the air, and that the once despised earth from which it drew its nourishment was its true parent and source of life.

Out of respect to its former protection and beauty, its owner had its wood made into handsome ornaments and seats for the garden to keep its memory alive in the minds of the children.

When any of them repined in after years at the lot which God had assigned them, the folly of the tree was alluded to, and all restlessness was allayed.

Over the spot where it stood a beautiful rustic basket made of its own wood was set, from which bright flowers blossomed throughout the summer day.

XI.
THE TWO WAYS.

Two men were informed, as they were listlessly standing and gazing into a dense forest one day, that beyond it lay a fertile and beautiful valley, reached only through the dark and close woods; but, when reached, it would repay them for all their efforts.

They started one morning, entering the forest together, and forced their way for a while through the tangled woods. They held the branches for each other to pass, and walked along in social converse. Soon one began to grow restless and impatient of the slow progress made.

"I must get on faster than this," he exclaimed, and began to quicken his pace, regardless of overhanging boughs and thorny branches, which pierced his flesh at every step. He rushed forward, leaving his companion; and, so intent did he become on reaching the valley with all possible speed, that he no longer noticed the briers which pierced him or the underbrush which entangled and made his feet sore. In a few days he reached the valley, tired, worn, and bleeding from head to feet.

The laborers who were working in their gardens looked on him with pity, and several, at the command of a leader, carried him to a house (for he could no longer walk), where he was cared for and nursed.

His companion, whom he had outrun, took a better and wiser course. Finding the wood so dense, he bethought himself of making a pathway as he journeyed. It would take much longer, but the comfort and good to others who might follow could not be told. Faithfully he labored, cutting away the branches which impeded his progress, and clearing the underbrush from the ground; while each day, in the valley beyond, the wounded man wondered that he came not, and concluded that he must have perished in the forest.

The days passed into weeks, and yet no sign of his companion. If he could only rise from his bed, he would go in search of him; but, alas! he was helpless, lame, and sore in every joint.

At the close of a beautiful autumn day, when the laborers had bound their sheaves and were going to their homes, a traveler was seen coming with a firm step from the forest. On his shoulder he carried the axe, whose polished edge glittered strangely in the rays of the setting sun. The laborers wondered why he was not torn and weary like the other.

"Thee must have had a better path than the one who came before thee," said one of the group to the stranger.

"I made a path," was his only answer; and then he glanced around the room, as though he would find him with whom he started: for the interest felt for any companionship, however brief, is not easily laid aside.

The laborers told him of his companion's inability to work, and of his days of pain.

"Let me see him," he said; and they went with him.

The next day the traveler who had slowly journeyed, and made a path for those who would come after, was able to go to his labors; while his companion was disabled for many days longer.

Soon after, many others came through the forest to the valley, and their first remark was, "Show us the traveler who made for us such a comfortable path;" and, seeing him, they all blessed him in word and deed for his nobleness in making their way so easy for them.

"But for that path," said many to him, "I should never have come to this lovely valley."

There are two ways of journeying through life: one, like the first pilgrim, who thought only of self and of speedily reaching the vale and the journey's end; the other better and wiser one, productive of greater good to all, of making a path, that all who come after us may be blessed by our labors.

XII.
THE URNS.

In a peaceful valley there lived a number of people whose leader dwelt on the hill and guided the tillers of the soil, weaving into their lives many lessons of truth. They were supplied with water from the mountain, which was sent them every morning by a carrier. It was the master's rule that each should have his urn clean, that the fresh supply might not be mingled with the old. For a time all were faithful: as each day's supply was used the urn was made clean for the new. But, alas for human weakness! so prone to fall from the line of duty--soon a murmur was heard among the people.

"I have had no fresh water for days," said one of the group standing idly by the roadside.

"Neither have I," said another.

"It's no use for the master to expect us to labor," remarked a third, "if we are not supplied with fresh water. Life is hard enough to bear with all we can have to help us," he continued. "Now there's our neighbor, Cheerful, over the way--his urn is full of pure, sparkling water each morning."

"And why?" broke in a voice in tones of remonstrance. The idlers looked at each other, and then at the face of old Faithful, who was just returning from his evening walk and had heard their words of complaint.

"Let me assure you, my neighbors," he said mildly, yet with force, "it's all your own fault that your urns are not filled. You each know the master's command, that they should be kept clean and ready for the fresh supply. Have you all been faithful to the command?"

They thought among themselves, and answered with but partial truth, saying, "We may not always have had our urns clean, but why should they be unfilled for that?"

"Because the new water would be made unclean and useless by being mixed with the old, as you each can see for yourselves. Our master loves all alike; but he cannot supply us with fresh waters and new life if we have not used the old and prepared for the new."

"I suppose, if we had them ever so clean now, that the carrier would pass us by," remarked one of the group.

"Try, and see," said Faithful. "We may always rest assured that if our part is done the master will do his; for no one, however kind and merciful, can benefit us if we do not put ourselves in a state to be blessed. If the master sends us fresh water each day, and our urns are impure, is it the fault of the benefactor that they are so? We must prepare to receive."

Faithful went on his way. The sun sank in its bed of fleecy clouds, the evening dew fell on the earth, and all was still. The lesson must have penetrated the hearts of the listeners; for on the morrow their urns, white and clean, were full of sparkling water.

Do we look into our hearts each day and see that the life from thence has gone forth for good and made ready for new, or are we idly murmuring that we have no life-waters? Can the Father's life inflow if we do not *give*? Our souls are sacred urns, which He longs to fill to overflowing with pure and heavenly truths if we are willing to receive, and faithful to extend, his mercies.

XIII.
SELF-EXERTION.

An aged man who had built for himself a house upon a high elevation of land, and had labored many years, yea, the most of his lifetime, in conveying trees, plants, and flowers with which to decorate his grounds, came one day in his descent upon a youth who sat by the roadside looking greatly dispirited.

"Hast thou no parents nor home?" inquired the kind man.

The youth shook his head, and looked so lonely and sad that the heart of the questioner was touched, and he said, "Come with me."

The boy looked pleased at the invitation, and, springing to his feet, stood by the stranger.

Together they commenced the long and toilsome ascent; but the feet of the youth were tender, and ere long the aged man was obliged to carry him on his back to the very summit.

He set his burden down at the door of his pleasant home, expecting to see an expression of wonder or pleasure on the boy's face; but only a sensuous look of satisfaction at the comforts which the laborer had gathered about him was visible on his dull features.

"I'll let him rest to-night," said the kind man. "To-morrow he shall have his first lesson in weeding the beds and watering the flowers."

At dawn the old man arose, dressed himself, and went forth to view the sun as it rose over the hills; while the youth slumbered on till nearly noon, and when he arose manifested no life nor interest till the evening meal was over. He partook largely of the bounties, and seemed so full of animation that the old man took courage, and smiles of satisfaction settled on his features; for he thought he had found a helper for himself and wife.

The next day they called him at sunrise, and after many efforts succeeded in arousing him from his sleep. The aged couple went to their garden after the morning meal, and awaited the appearance of the youth.

"I sent him to gather ferns to plant beside these rocks: he surely cannot be all this time gathering them," remarked the woman.

The husband went to the edge of the wood whither she had sent him, and found him lying upon the ground, looking dreamingly at the skies.

The good couple did not succeed in arousing him to a sense of any duty. He was dead to labor, and had no life to contribute to the scene around him.

"I fear you have made a mistake," said the wife of the good man when the shadows of evening came and they were alone. "I see the boy can never appreciate the toil of our years. He must return and climb the mount for himself. He has no appreciation of all this accumulation which we have been years in gaining, nor can he have. It is not in the order of life: each must climb the summit himself. A mistake lies in our taking any one in our arms and raising him to the mount."

"I see it now," said her husband, who had, like many people, been more kind than wise, and like many foolish parents who injure their offspring by giving them the result of their years of toil.

On the morrow, the youth was sent back. A few years after, the aged man saw him toiling up a steep hill, seeking to make a home of his own. It was a beautiful eminence, and overlooked the fields and woods for miles around.

"He will know the worth and comfort of it," said the old man to his companion.

"Toil and sacrifice will make it a sweet spot," she answered; "and after the morning of labor will come the evening of rest."

XIV.
THE VINES.

They grew side by side. The most casual observer would have said that one was far more beautiful than the other. Its height was not only greater, but its foliage was brighter.

"I should think," remarked the vine of superior external appearance to the other, "that, for the gardener's sake, you would try and make a better appearance. I heard him remark this morning that he almost despaired of your ever bearing fruit, or looking even presentable. I am sure we each have the same soil to draw our nourishment from, and one hand to prune away our deformities."

"I think I can defend myself to the satisfaction of both yourself and the gardener; and if you will listen to me this evening, as I cannot spare any of the moments of the day, I will tell you what labor occupies so much of my time."

"Both myself and the gardener would be delighted to have an explanation; for it has been a wonder to us both what you can be doing. You certainly have not attained any height, nor put forth foliage of any account for the past year."

The full-leaved vine spent the day fluttering her leaves in the wind and listening to the praise of passers-by.

"What a difference in these vines!" exclaimed two gentlemen as they walked past the garden.

"Just what every one remarks," said the good-looking vine to herself; and, raising her head very high in the air, she put forth another shoot. Yet, with all her fullness of conceit and vainglory, she grew very impatient for the hour to arrive when her sister would be at leisure to talk with her.

At sunset, after the gardener had laid his tools away and closed the garden gates for the evening, her sister announced to her that she was ready to explain her strange life for the past year.

"If you can call anything 'life' which has no visible sign of growth or motion," pertly remarked the gay vine.

Her sister took no notice of the remark, though it wounded her, and some of her leaves fluttered and fell to the ground. Had her sister been more sensitive, she could have seen her tremble in every limb, though her voice was sweet and clear as she commenced, saying, "I have been very busy the past year, but in a direction which no one but myself could perceive. Knowing that we are subject to periods of drought, I have been, and I think wisely too, occupying all my time in sending fibres into the earth in every direction. I have already got one as far as the brook, the other side of the wall. I heard the gardener say it was never dry, so I struck out in that direction, and expect to bring forth fruit next year for all."

"But could you not have put forth some leaves, at least, and made a more pleasing appearance?" inquired her sister.

"No: it took all my strength to strike into the earth. I hope to see the time when no one will be ashamed of my appearance."

The vain vine grew quite thoughtful. Was she, after all, ahead of her sister? Was a good external appearance the sure sign of merit?

These questions kept her busy for many days. She reasoned them in her mind, but did not act on the lesson they taught. She, too, would like to have made preparation for seasons of drought, but her pride stood in the way. She feared to lose her lovely foliage; and the month sped on.

Another year came. The earth was parched: no rain fell on the dry plants and leaves. The once lovely vine lost all her foliage, while her sister was full of leaves and promise of fruit.

"I declare," said the gardener, "it does seem strange. I expected this vine had lost all its life; yet it is now bright and vigorous, while the one I looked to for much fruit is fast fading. What can be the reason?"

Later in the season, the vine which had worked so long out of sight had the pleasure of seeing not only the table of its owner supplied with delicious fruits from its branches, but also of hearing the gardener remark to visitors that the sick and feeble of the neighborhood were strengthened and refreshed by the cooling grapes which she had, through so much exertion brought forth.

The other vine bore no fruit, and had to be pruned severely; but pride stood no longer in the way of her progress. She began to send forth her fibres into the earth, as her sister had done. It was hard at first for her to be obliged to listen to the praises of one whom she considered her inferior; but she at length attained that glorious height which enables us to rejoice when the earth has been made richer, no matter by whom or by what means.

XV.
IN THE WORLD.

A parent who loved his son more wisely than most earthly parents, and who longed to see him crowned with the light of wisdom, felt that he must send him afar from himself to gather immortal truth: and his heart was moved with a deeper grief at the thought that he must send him forth alone, and unprovided with means to procure his daily sustenance; for only thus could he learn the lessons which were necessary for his soul's development.

The boy lay sleeping upon a soft white bed: his hands were folded peacefully upon his breast. Hard was the task the father knew was his,--to break that sleep, that slumber so profound, and send his boy out into a cold and selfish world. But, shaking off the tremor and the weakness of his soul, he said, "Arise, my son: I must send you forth upon a long and dangerous journey to gather truths to light your soul; and you must go without the means to procure your bread and shelter. It grieves my heart, my son, that all this must be so; but yet I know the journey must be taken, and all its dangers and privations met. My prayers and blessings will go with you, child, through all your scenes."

The astonished son gazed on his father's face. The parent turned and wept; then, wiping away the fast-falling tears, he said, "I do not wonder at your earnest, curious gaze, you who have so long lived in the bosom of my love; but there are lessons that must be learned by every human soul. I cannot tell you what these lessons are: they must be experienced, else gladly would I spare you the toil, and myself the pain of parting."

The boy looked sad as he thought of the perils and exposures to which he should be subjected, without means to procure the least comfort.

The night shades fell on the earth. Only a glimmer of daylight tinged the sky when father and son parted, the one for action, the other to endure and wait his return.

The journey for many days lay over cheerless hills and barren plains; and many a tear was brushed from that young cheek by the hand which his father had so warmly pressed at parting.

At the close of a dark, stormy day, weary and faint for food, he was about to lie down on the damp grass, overcome with weariness, when he espied an elegant edifice a little way beyond.

"I will travel on," he said hopefully; "for surely, in such a mansion, I shall find protection and food for my famished body."

It took much longer to reach it than he expected; but at last, with torn and bleeding feet, he came to the broad avenue which led to the dwelling.

"What magnificence!" he exclaimed. "How glad I am that my father sent me hither to see such wondrous things!" With hope beaming in every feature, he approached the door and knocked.

It was opened by one whose voice and face exhibited no sign of welcome. He cast an impatient glance upon the traveler, who shrank abashed and trembling from so rude a gaze.

"Can I find food and shelter here?" he asked, his voice tremulous with emotion.

The door was shut upon him.

It was not the cold of the piercing storm which he felt then, but the chill of an inhospitable soul. It froze the warm current of hope that, a few moments before, had leaped so wildly in his veins; and he went forth from the elegant mansion, and sat upon the ground and wept.

"O father! why did you send your child so far away to meet the harsh and cruel treatment of the world when your home abounds with plenty?" said the weary child.

The shades of night were gathering fast. The cold, damp ground, which had been his only bed so many nights, offered a poor protection now for his weary form.

"I was contented there. Why did he send me hither?" was the questioning of his mind as he sat alone and sad.

As he was about to lay himself upon the ground, he saw light glimmering through the trees, just as the light of hope breaks on us at the moment of despair.

"I would journey thither," he said, despondingly; "but rest and shelter were denied me here. How can I hope to find it elsewhere?"

But hope whispered to his weary heart; and he arose, and passed on.

It was a small, humble dwelling, but one in which dwelt loving hearts.

He turned involuntarily into the little path that wound by fragrant shrubs and flowers to its door, and then checked himself, as though he could not bear again a cold denial. It were far easier to feel the blast and storm than again to hear unwelcome tones fall on his ears. Despite his feeble faith, he walked to the door and gave a timid rap.

The door flew open wide, as though the hinges were oiled with love; and there stood before him a form all radiant with smiles of welcome. She bade him enter; and the traveler, already warm with her bright smiles and words of welcome, felt a glow pervade his whole being,--a feeling new and unfelt before; for he had never, before this absence from his father's house, known a want or woe.

Both food and shelter did the woman give unto him; and, when the morning sun came over the eastern hills, another sun of joy and gratitude was shining over his hills of doubt. And when the woman turned from his warm, full thanks, and went about her daily tasks, these words came with a new life and meaning to her mind: "As ye have done it to the least of these my brethren, ye have done it unto me."

Years rolled away. The murmur of their deeds was like the distant rumbling of retreating clouds after a great storm.

The youth visited strange cities, saw nations at war with each other, and learned the conflict of the human soul, and how it battles in the great life which threatens to bear it down each hour. Amid all this strife and selfishness of heart, he found many that were loyal to God and Truth. He daily learned rich lessons which he would not have effaced for all the gold and pomp of earth.

The light of wisdom began to dawn. "This is the experience which my father saw I needed. Had he provided me with means with which to journey through the world, how different would have been my life! I then should have known no value of human love and kindness. O my father! I long to return to thee, and love thee as I never could have loved thee before!"

He sat weary, but not sad, by the roadside one day, thinking of his father's love, when the sound of a traveler's approach was heard on the road. He turned his eyes in its direction, and saw one of his father's servants on a beautiful white horse.

"Your father bids you come," were the welcome words that fell upon his ears.

"Take thy steed," he said, "and journey quickly home: he waits impatiently for your return."

Fast over hill and dale he rode; and when day passed from sight, leaving a jeweled sky to mark its absence, the long-absent son rode to his father's door, and wept tears of joy upon his breast.

Together they stood, father and son, upon the Mount of Experience, overlooking all the scenes of life.

Our heavenly Father wakes us all from the slumber of infancy and helplessness, and sends us forth alone into the world to learn life's great lessons. When we have learned them well, he sends the pale messenger, Death, to take us home. How blessed will be that reunion! With the crown of wisdom on our heads, how sweet it will be to go no more out, but dwell with him forever!

XVI.
FAITH, HOPE, AND CHARITY.

In one of the dark periods, when shadows lay upon the earth, a beautiful angel was sent to abide there and teach the doubting and weary of a Father's love and care.

She found it a tedious task, and, after many years of toil, felt that she needed a helper.

"If my sister were here," she often said to the people, "she could aid you to greater efforts; for, while I seem to supply a needed element to your souls, I only half succeed in meeting your wants."

"If she is but half as good as yourself we will welcome her," answered those to whom she spoke.

"I will go for her," said Faith, one dark night, after she had been trying to rouse the people to higher states, with what seemed to her but little success. Faith was weary, and wept; and, when her tears flowed, her sister, yet in the realms of peace, by a strange law of sympathy, knew it, and ran to her father, saying, "I, too, must go to the earth; for Faith needs me."

Her parent sat awhile in deep thought, and Hope waited impatiently for his answer, which came spoken in a firm, clear voice: "We have done Faith a great wrong, I fear, in sending her alone where so much light and comfort is needed. It was too much for her. Go, Hope, and my blessing attend you."

She was overjoyed at receiving her father's permission to join her sister; for, since Faith had gone, her beautiful home had seemed lonely.

Faith sat all night with her eyes uplifted to heaven, and, when the morning sun lit the hill-tops, behold! on its beams Hope was descending to earth.

Faith was not long in ascending the hill to meet her sister. Their meeting was full of joy.

"If my eyes had not been lifted heavenward, I should have missed you, Hope: and you must have searched a long time for me; for my journeys are far each day," said Faith to her sister.

"Keep your eyes *ever* uplifted," answered Hope, "and you will see not only the brightness of the heavens, but also the father's angels whom he chooses to send to your aid."

"I will," answered Faith; and ever after her eyes were raised heavenward.

They descended to the valley, hand in hand, and reached it as the people were passing to their daily toils.

How light now seemed the labors of Faith! What a comfort it was to have Hope by her when she walked along the dreary wayside; and Hope's bright words, how they cheered the downhearted!

"I wonder your parents ever permitted you to come to the earth alone," remarked an old and venerable woman to Faith, as the latter was imparting to her some truths which lay almost beyond the grasp of mortals.

"My father, as well as myself, had to learn that I needed Hope with me to make my work more perfect. We must first feel our own inadequacy before our helpers can be fully appreciated. I think she came in the right time," said Faith reverently.

"No doubt," replied the woman; "I have often heard you say that all our blessings come at the needful moment; but surely Hope looks as though she could endure the rough clime, and still rougher ways of our people, better than yourself, although I do not know what my life would have been without you."

"That was why I was sent here. I came to prepare the way for Hope. I was needed first; and now, with my sister's brighter element, I expect to do a good work on the earth."

"A blessed pair!" exclaimed the woman, as they left her home to go to others more dark and drear.

Faith was summoned that night to the home of a widow whose only child was passing away; for the clear, far-seeing eyes of Faith could see the soul depart and take on its heavenly form. It was a great comfort to the bereaved in hours like those to have her near.

"I wonder how we lived without her," were household words, and words which she could hear without any semblance of vainglory; for her soul was too deeply impressed with the magnitude of her mission to allow her to be elated or depressed by any remark that might be made.

Faith's eyes followed the dying boy far into the realms of light. She wiped the mother's tears away, and disclosed to her sight the way the soul had fled, while Hope stood by to assure her that the parting was not forever. The two tarried through the night with the mother, and when friends came to bury the dead form she had learned that "the grave is not the goal."

The sisters toiled together many years. They wove beautiful truths into the minds of the people, till the once dark condition of earth seemed passing rapidly away. People grew trustful, and less gloomy: yet, with all the teachings of Faith, and the cheering words of Hope, they failed to exercise the right feelings at all times towards each other.

The sisters sat by the wayside one evening, after a hard day's toil, their eyes lifted to the stars, which seemed to look lovingly on them. They sat without words, while each possessed the same unspoken wish. They both longed for their sister, who at that moment was thinking earnestly of them.

Faith glanced from the stars to the scarcely less brilliant eyes of Hope, and a few tears fell over her face. Even Hope sighed, and almost wished herself back to her starry home with her father.

"Are you sorry, Hope, that you came to earth?" asked Faith, tenderly.

"No: but I was thinking--"

"I know your thought: it must be the same as my own," said Faith.

"Yes, our sister--" Hope ventured thus far.

"Charity come too." Faith finished the sentence.

"Just my wish," said Hope, rejoiced to find they had the same desire.

"I see," said Faith, "that we are all needed here to make our work complete," while the brilliant eyes of Hope spoke more than words.

"I have felt for a long time," answered Hope, "that another element, softer, sweeter, and finer than ours, was needful for the people."

"Do you suppose that father would spare Charity, too?" asked Hope of her sister.

"I know he would, if convinced that earth's people would receive her."

"Why, Faith, you speak with such confidence!"

"Because I know how good our father is, as you do yourself, Hope. If needed, she will come," said Faith, trustingly, thinking of her own experience that lonely night.

"Charity is so delicate," said Hope, a little doubtfully, "I do not quite see how she could endure this cold clime."

"She could not without our presence to sustain her," answered Faith.

"But, with us to help her, she could; for we can all live wherever we are called to do the work of our father."

"Let us lift the voices of our souls," said Hope; and they offered a silent prayer for their sister.

*   *   *   *   *

That night, in his abode of peace and comfort, the father walked to and fro; for the voices of his children on the earth, pleading for their sister, had reached him.

It was not without a struggle that he called the only remaining child to his side to look upon her for the last time for many years.

"It must be," he said, "and then will my sacrifice be perfect; and from perfect sacrifice must fullness of good come forth. Faith alone could not perfect the work; Hope's added brightness was not all that was needed. Charity must be added." And he drew the fair, frail form to his side, and told her to go for her mantle.

He enveloped her slight figure in the spotless garment, and, placing her in the care of Zephyr, the gentle west wind, who was always faithful to her charges, bade her depart, with his prayers and blessings.

Zephyr was very tender of her charge, and, after what seemed a long journey to Charity, she laid her on a soft bed of moss in a pleasant woodland, where her sisters were gathering flowers.

She might have lain there some time had not Faith's eyes discovered her coming through the clouds.

Full and joyous was the meeting of the three; and when the sun went to rest they sought shelter among the people.

With the uplifted eyes of Faith, the clear, soul-speaking face of Hope, and the tender, forgiving words of Charity, their united force was great.

Some of the people at first refused to admit the last comer into their dwellings.

"Faith, with her lovely eyes, and Hope, with her bright ways, are good enough," they said; "and why need they bring this pale, fragile one to earth?"

But when once she had spoken, either in council or rebuke, to her listeners, there was melody and richness in her tones: such an awakening of their souls' finer powers that they ever after bade her welcome.

Her strength lay in her gentleness. She always went when called for, but never obtruded herself on others. Very often her sisters were invited to the feast of the people without her. It took time for her quality to be known: she was so still and silent. Her step, too, was noiseless, and her delicate feet left no prints where she trod.

Before she grew into favor with the people they used to watch for her footprints to see whose guest she had been; but they found no traces, and learned to entertain her after a long time for the lovely qualities which she possessed.

They walk the earth now, each loved and entertained by many, while some sit in the shadows, and know not that earth has the angels of Faith, Hope, and Charity to bless them.

XVII.
GOING FORTH.

A wise parent sent his children to a distant country to learn the lessons of life which experience alone can teach. Before their departure he called them to him, and, after providing them liberally with means, told them that at their return he would listen to their several experiences; at the same time telling them to use the means which he had given them well--neither to hoard, nor spend them unwisely; above all, not to bring them back in their original form, but a full equivalent therefore, either in spiritual or material things.

A year had scarcely passed, when, as the father sat looking at the western sky, the youngest son came running breathlessly up the path.

"So soon returned?" asked his father--which caused a look of disappointment to pass over the face of the youth; and his words were shaded with regret as he replied, "I thought you would be glad to see me, and would rejoice that I got through so quickly."

"Not so, my son," replied the father. "You cannot, in the brief time you have been absent, have performed many, if any, deeds of goodness compared with what you might have done by tarrying longer; and your gold--you surely cannot have used it all in so brief a period."

"Why, I've brought all the money back you gave me, father. You see, I got through without its costing me a penny."

"It grieves me more than all, my son, that you should go through any country and return no equivalent for deeds and kindness given. Rest awhile, and in a few days return to the land and the people I sent you among, and come not back again to me till every farthing is wisely spent."

The youth murmured within himself, but dared not reply. A few days later he departed, to go over the same ground and do the work he had neglected for the sake of a speedy return.

At the end of the second year another returned, looking sad and dispirited.

"Thou hast soon returned, my son," said the father. "Is thy work done in so brief a period?"

The youth hung his head, and answered slowly, "I was so weary, father. I saw so much sorrow among those people, I longed to come home where all is rest and peace. Surely, I was right in that, was I not?"

"Far from it, my child. If there was much sorrow there, that was the very reason why you should have remained. Dost thou not remember those lines I have so often quoted,--

"'Rest is not quitting the busy career: Rest is the fitting of self to one's sphere'?"

"I remember them well, father," the youth replied; "but I never felt their meaning until now."

"And if you sense it now, my son, what is your duty?"

"To return, I suppose."

"But how--cheerfully or otherwise?"

"Gladly and willingly," said the son, born from the old to the higher self.

"I will provide you with more means," remarked his father, while a feeling of joy thrilled his being at the thought that his son was going to give his life to human needs.

They parted on the morrow, though that separation was the nearest approach of their lives; for they were united by a truth which is ever the essence of a divine union. Many years passed by. The hair of the father grew whiter, and his ears longed to hear the voices of his sons, yet he would not call, in word or feeling, so long as the busy throng was receiving or giving them life.

One evening, when his thoughts were taking a somewhat pensive turn, a messenger came to his door with a letter from the long-absent and eldest, who had not returned to his home since the day of his departure. Its words were these:--

"Dear Father,--I cannot come to the home I love so well, nor to your side, while this land is so full of need of human words and deeds. With your blessing I shall remain here my lifetime; and when age comes on, and I can no longer serve the people, may I return?"

The tears fell over the good man's face. God had blessed him greatly in bestowing on him so worthy a son; and he penned warm and glowing words of encouragement to his child, and sent by the messenger, with gold to alleviate the wants of the needy.

"Tell him a thousand blessings await him when his work is done," said he to the messenger as the latter mounted his horse to ride away.

Long after, when the father grew old and helpless, the sons returned laden with rich experiences and abundantly able to care for him.

They had learned the great and valuable lesson that all must learn ere they truly live,--that we must give to receive, sow if we would reap, and lose our life to find it.

XVIII.
THE FEAST.

There was once a husbandman who had laborers in a valley, clearing it of stones and brush, that it might become fit for culture. He resided near, on a fine hill, where he raised rare fruits and flowers of every variety. The view from the hill-top was extensive and grand beyond description, and it was the kind owner's desire that each day the laborers should ascend and be refreshed by whatever he had to offer them, beside catching the inspiration of the lovely and extensive landscape. Some days he had not much to offer them; at other times, the repast would be sumptuous and most tempting: so those who went each day were sure of receiving in their season the delicious fruits which ripened at different periods.

There had been a succession of days in which there was nothing but dry food on the hill, with none of the luscious fruits which invigorate and refresh; for they had been slow in ripening, and the kind husbandman would not gather them before they were mellow and fit to spread before his laborers.

"*I* am not going to climb the hill to-day for a few crumbs," said one dissatisfied toiler, as he sat by the roadside at noon-day, looking very unhappy.

"Nor I!" "Nor I!" added a second and a third, until there was quite a chorus of the dissatisfied.

The remainder went up as usual. A most tempting repast was before them, of fruits and cake and refreshing wines, while the table was decked with rare and fragrant flowers.

How glad was the good man to spread the bounties before them! for well he knew of the murmurs which had gone out of their hearts for a few days past. "Are they not all here?" he asked of those who had ascended the hill, while a look of disappointment came over his face.

"Oh! let us go down and tell them what a nice feast is waiting," said one of the group, as he gazed on the well-filled table.

"Nay, not so," answered the husbandman, in a gentle but commanding tone. "My people should have faith in me, and know that I spread for them all I can each day. My power, even like that of the Infinite, is limited by conditions. It is not my pleasure ever to have them go unrefreshed; but how much better for them, could they be content with whatever comes each day, though sometimes meager. How it cheers me to see those who have come in good courage and faith, ***not*** knowing that the feast was here. Eat and give thanks," he said; while a band played some lively airs.

*　　*　　*　　*　　*

Shall we refuse to ascend each day the mount whereon dwells our Father? Shall we, because some days no feast awaits us, linger in the valley of doubt, and lose the bounties which his hand at other times has ready for us? No: the faithful and believing will go up to the mount each day, and take without murmur the morsel, or the fruits with thanksgiving.

XIX.
THE LESSON OF THE STONE.

It was with feelings of satisfaction and pride that a builder looked upon a large and costly edifice which, after much exertion, was just completed. Long had the workmen toiled to place one stone upon another. Many hours of thought had the designer spent in perfecting its proportions, and a deep sense of relief came over him as he saw the last stone deposited on the summit of the structure. Yet it was only to be followed by one of pain; for, as he walked one evening to enjoy the beautiful symmetry of his building, he heard words of contention and strife among the various stones of which it was composed.

"Just look at my superior finish," said one of the top pieces to those beneath it. "You are only plain pieces of granite, while I am polished, elegantly carved, and the admiration of all eyes. Do I not see all the people, as they pass by, look up at me?"

"Not so fast," replied one of the foundation stones. "A little less pride would become you; for do you not see that, but for us below, you could not be so high? And it matters very little, it strikes me, what part of the building we are placed in, if we but remain firm and peaceful."

The words of the wise stone pleased the owner so much that he resolved to remove a little of the vanity of the top one, and lay awake a long time that night, thinking of some plan by which to effect his purpose. The elements, however, spared him any effort on his part, for the next day a terrible hail-storm swept over the land, and its hard stones defaced all the ornaments which had led the lofty one to boast so loudly of its superiority.

"Oh, dear! oh, dear!" moaned the vain piece of granite. "How I wish I had been taken for a foundation stone, instead of being here to have all my beauty destroyed by this awful storm! I'd much rather have been in the middle of the building than up here, where all the force of the storm is spent on my head."

The stone at the foundation could not help smiling, though he really pitied the vain thing above him. "It will teach her wisdom," he said to himself; "and she may learn that none in life are lowly if they bear their part, and that a lofty position is far more dangerous than a humble one."

There was a fearful crash in the air at that instant. The foundation stone thought the building was coming down. Something struck him, which he recognized as a part of the top stone; for he had seen the workmen cutting and smoothing it day after day for many weeks prior to its elevation. Now she could boast no more of superior finish or position.

The following day, the remaining shattered portion was removed and left by the roadside, where it could see another prepared to take its place.

"I thought that stone was a little weak when we raised it," said one of the workmen as it was placed aside.

It lay by the roadside until it grew to be humble and glad to be of any use,--even delighted when one day the owner of the building took it to finish a wall which was being built around some pasture land.

"Here I can be of use," she said, as the workmen deposited it on a sunny corner as the place it was to occupy. It was glad to be there and find itself useful and at rest; for it had been obliged to listen to the remarks of the passers-by each day, and to endure their comments on its misfortune.

"I suppose I shall never know any other life but this; so now, being firmly set, I can sleep a little:" for the stone was sadly in need of rest.

After what seemed to be a long period of repose, the stone awoke, with new pulsations and finer emotions thrilling within it. The sound of children's voices were heard in the air. How sweet and life-giving they were! far more pleasant than the words of admiration which men uttered when she was on the building's top. A new joy was hers also, for soft hands were caressing her. Beautiful mosses had grown on her surface, and delighted children were gathering them.

Useful and beautiful too! and the stone was silent with happiness. She hoped the children would come again; and they did, bringing others with them.

"I wonder how this beautiful moss grew on me," she said one day to herself--at least she thought no one heard her. But an older stone beside her replied, "By being perfectly quiet we become covered with this lovely moss, firmer than grasses of any lawn."

The once vain stone grew to be perfectly contented, and never longed for her former position. When the storms came, it knew it was close to the earth. It had no fearful height to be pulled from, and the beautiful lichens which grew upon its surface were far more ornamental than its former carved and elegant adornings.

XX.
THE SEEDS.

They lay side by side one morning, while the gardener was preparing the ground in which to plant them and many other varieties.

"Just think," said the more talkative one of the two, "how sad it is that we are going to be put in that dismal ground! I shall not allow myself to be buried out of sight this lovely morning."

"But," answered the more quiet seed by her side, "it is only for a brief period that we shall lie there, and then we shall be far more beautiful."

"What care I for beauty for others to look at? I want my freedom, and intend to have it, too. The wind is my friend, and I shall ask her to waft me over to those lovely hills, where I can see something of the world."

"I think it would be wiser to remain where we are, and let the gardener care for us: he must know what is for our good," remarked the gentle seed.

"You are too prosy by far. I think our own feelings tell us what we need. So good-by," exclaimed the self-reliant seed, as she motioned to the wind to bear her away.

She thought her breath was leaving her, as she was borne through the air, and wished she were back in the garden. But when she found herself on the warm hill-side she felt reassured, and nestled herself amid the soft grass, whose waving motion soon lulled her to sleep.

Now the two seeds which the gardener had laid on the ground were of a very choice and rare kind; and he felt very sad that the wind should have blown one away. He took the remaining one and laid it carefully in the ground, with many hopes that it would spring up and bear rich blossoms, which would yield more seed. That night a cold wind came on; but the little seed in the warm bed did not feel it at all, while her absent sister shook all night with the cold.

After what seemed a long time to the seed in the ground, something like a new life came over her. There was a deeper pulsation through her being, and a strong desire to shoot upward to the light and air. This feeling deepened every hour.

"At this rate I shall soon be in the air, where I can see all that is going on about me," she said joyfully. Then she felt very quiet, and fell asleep. When she awoke she saw the gardener bending over her with a joyful face. "When did this happen? How came I up here in the warm sunlight?" the seed exclaimed to him.

"Because the wind did not bear you away, and I could put you in the ground, is the reason why you are here. First out of sight, then to the light, my little seed! But," he said sorrowfully, "I wish we had the other one, for your kind is rare."

The plant then told the gardener that her sister purposely went away, at which he wondered that she had power of motion until she became a plant.

"Oh, she asked the wind to carry her," answered the fresh-growing plant.

"If I knew where she had gone I'd search for her, and bring her back."

"She asked the wind to take her to yonder hill-side," said the plant, hoping, oh, so much! that he would go and find the seed, and plant it beside her, that she, too, might have the pleasure of becoming a plant as beautiful as herself.

The gardener went towards the hills; but the seed saw him, and begged the south wind to bear her away. And she took her on her wing and wafted her many miles from home.

The gardener searched a long time, and was obliged to return without her. So he took extra care of the plant, and it grew to be the pride of the garden; while the seed that had her own way was roaming over the world. The truant one soon lost all her influence over the winds, who finally refused to carry about a good-for-nothing seed while they had so much needful work to perform. A cold northern blast was the last one she could persuade to bear her, and he dropped her on a rock, where she at last perished from exposure to the rain and cold.

The day before her death, a company of people passed by her, bearing in their hands some rare and fragrant blossoms, to which she felt a strange attraction. This gave place to a deep thrill of sorrow as she heard them describe the lovely plant which grew in a beautiful garden, and which by their description she knew was her own home, which she in her folly had left.

"Had I but accepted the conditions of growth, I too might have been a lovely plant, giving and receiving pleasure," she said, after the people had passed on. "But now, alas!" and her breath grew quick and short, "if I had only some one to profit by my last words, telling of my life of folly, I might not have lived wholly in vain." But there was nothing about her which she could discern save a tuft of moss upon the cold, hard rock which must now be her death-bed.

But behind the rock, on the south side, there was growing a family of wild daisies, who were going to migrate to a warmer part of the country to plant their seeds before the winter came on. This was one of the conditions which Providence ever has around the most seemingly deserted and desolate, that her words might not only profit them, but that they could convey the benefit of them to all wayward seeds who were unwilling to accept the natural conditions of growth. And thus the seed, though dying with its mission unfulfilled, did not live wholly in vain; for its wasted life saved others from a similar fate.

XXI.
ONLY GOLD.

A parent sent his children forth one day into a fertile land to gather fruits, flowers, and whatever was beautiful to adorn their homes. They wandered till nightfall, gathering their treasures, while their joyous laughter filled the air, and made music to the listening laborers in the fields.

Just as the shadows of evening came on they approached an open field: it was barren of verdure, but the ground was covered with golden stones, which glittered strangely in the setting sun. They gathered as many as they could with their other treasures, and then all but one of the group began to prepare for home, while he lingered, eager to gather the shining pebbles.

"We must return," they all said in chorus to him. They disliked to leave without him; but darkness was fast coming on, and they must obey their parents' command and return before the shades of evening had covered the earth. One voice after another died away on the air as they pleaded vainly for him to go with them, but he heeded them not: the golden stones were far more precious in his eyes than kindred, home, or friends; and they departed sorrowfully without him, while he remained and added stone to stone, till he was obliged at last, from exhaustion, to lie down on the damp ground.

It was not like his warm bed in his pleasant home; and he missed the cheerful voices of his brothers, and more than all his parents' fond goodnight, after the evening prayer. He slept; but his dreams were wild and feverish, and there was no atmosphere of love about him to soothe the weary brain.

The next day at noon his parents sent a messenger to him, bidding him return. But the love of his golden stones was paramount to the wishes of kindred, and the unnumbered comforts of a happy home; and his reply to the messenger was, "I will return, when I have enough of these," pointing to a large collection which was already higher than his head. At nightfall hunger seized him. He felt too weary to go in search of food, but the demand of nature asserted its claim, and he dragged himself to a field near by, where grew berries and fruits in abundance. His spirits rose after the cravings of hunger were satisfied, and he lay down again by his precious pile of stones.

The days glided into weeks, and still he fed upon the berries and gathered the golden pebbles. His father had ceased to send messengers to him, knowing that nothing but a long experience would teach his child the value of life's many blessings, and that gold *alone* has no power to bless us. The father suffered much in knowing and realizing that his son must learn the truths of life through such severe lessons; but wisdom told him it could not be otherwise.

The chill air of autumn came, and no longer could the fruits and berries ripen for him. He saw some laborers one day in a field near by, eating their meal which they had brought from their homes. Oh; what would he not now give for some of their meat and bread! "I will go to them," he said, "and offer some of my golden stores in exchange for just a few morsels."

He did so; and they only smiled at his offer, saying, "What would then refresh and fit us for the rest of our day's labor? Surely your gold would not."

"But it would help you to buy more," he replied.

"Yes, to-morrow: but we cannot spare a morsel to-day, for we need all our supply to strengthen us for our work."

He turned away in deep thought. Was he not losing all of life's joys and comforts in living thus alone only to amass such quantities of gold? But as he looked again on the shining treasures his ambition arose with increased power; and he forgot, for a time, his hunger in his toil. Then a new thought came to him. "Now that the fruits are gone I can go to the forest and gather nuts. They will be better food, too, for these chilly autumn days. Surely I am provided for, at least till winter," and he left his labor and repaired to the woods, where he feasted and gathered enough for many days.

The household mourned much for their absent brother. They missed him in their daily joys, and every hour they watched, waited, and hoped to see him return. They almost rejoiced when the bleak winds of autumn swept the foliage from the trees, because they could look farther down the road for their brother.

"I shall soon be able to travel and see the world," said the youth to himself every day as the pile of gold grew higher; but, alas for human calculation! he awoke one morning to find his huge mountain of gold one solid mass. The action of the light, heat, and atmosphere had fused them together, and no exertion of his could break off even the smallest atom.

Must he return with not even one golden pebble? for he had gathered them all--not one was in sight, no more were to be found.

His golden dream of travel was over, and, worse, the freshness and buoyancy of youth had departed. His limbs, alas! were stiff and sore. He had a mountain of gold, not one atom of which he could use for himself or others. And now he must return to his father's house empty-handed, and void of truths or incidents to relate to his brothers.

But some kind angel led him home, where his blessings were yet in store, awaiting his return. One evening when the shadows crept over the earth, he walked up the well-known path. The brothers had long before ceased to watch for his coming; and great was their surprise to see him again among them, although not the brother of that happy, sunny day of long ago. He told them sadly of the result of his long toil, while they related to him the good results of their few golden pebbles, which they brought home, and with which their father had purchased land, which was now yielding them rich returns, aside from the health and pleasure which they derived from its culture, the labor of which they performed with their own hands. "Health, wealth, and happiness combined," he murmured sadly, as he felt keenly that his youth and opportunities had departed.

Are there not too many who seek for gold alone, forgetting the joys which it purchases, and forgetting that its possession alone has no value? Rightly acquired and used it alleviates and mediates, but gathered and amassed for itself only it is but a mountain of shining ore, valueless and unsatisfying to its possessor.

"Fool that I have been thus to waste my time and strength!" said the long-absent son that night as his father bade him welcome.

"If wisdom is purchased by the experience, it matters not how great the price," answered his parent.

"But I have lost my youth and my strength," responded the son.

"Which loss will be compensated by more thought and greater ability to labor mentally," said his parent consolingly.

In after years the youth who had wasted his bodily strength became a worker in words of cheer and hope to others, and hence he had not wholly lived in vain. He learned to love the angel Truth so well that she came to his side each day, and gave him sweet counsel and many lessons for mankind.

But he had purchased the light at a cost which few can afford to give.

XXII.
THE SACRIFICE.

A large party of travelers on their way to a distant country were obliged to pass through a dense forest to reach it. Their leader went forward, and, seeing the darkness of the dense woods, was convinced of the impossibility of his people going through it, without the aid of a light to guide them. He sat beside the mossy stones at the entrance, trying to devise some means by which to light up the darkness. There seemed but one way, and that almost hopeless, as it involved a sacrifice of life, and he knew too well the nature of the trees to expect any of them to give themselves up for his travelers. How could he ask it, as he stepped into the deep wood, and looked on their grand proportions and rich foliage? His was no enviable position to entreat them to give up the existence which must be dear to themselves,--to pass from the known to the unknown life.

Vainly he tried to think of another way to accomplish his purpose. None presented itself; so with glowing words he appealed to their nobler selves, telling them all the great need of the travelers who were obliged to pass that way. First he appealed to a fine birch which bordered the forest.

"Not I, indeed!" answered the tree. "Do you think I would give my life to light a few people through this woodland? I prefer to live a few years longer."

He next addressed a walnut. She shook a few leaves from her branches, and made a similar reply, preferring to live in her own form, and amid her sister trees, to going she knew not whither.

"Are there none here," he continued, "who are willing to sacrifice their lives for the needs of others?"

He looked around the forest in vain: all were silent, and he was about to return to the people, when a large and stately oak spoke in clear and ringing tones, saying,

"I will give my body that the travelers may have light."

"What! that grand old body of yours, that has been so many years growing and maturing to its present stately and fair proportions!" exclaimed several of the trees.

"You are not only rash, but foolish," remarked a small fir growing by its side.

"Beside taking away the pride of our grand old forest," said a delicate birch, that had always admired the oak.

"Just throwing your life away," broke in a tall and rather sickly pine.

"When will you be ready for me?" asked the oak of the leader, who had stood admiring its beautiful proportions, and sorrowing within himself that it must be so.

At the close of the next day the travelers came to the edge of the forest, and tarried while their leader lit the fire at the roots of the oak. Now the flames went upward and flashed in the darkness; for it was evening, and not a star was visible. The flames rose upward and touched not even the bark of another tree, but wound closely around the oak, as though it knew its work and that the light of that tree only was needed to pass the travelers through in safety. It touched their hearts to thus witness that the life of the noble oak must be sacrificed, and they offered, with one accord, a silent prayer that its life might be extended in a higher form. Having passed through, they tarried at the end of the forest until the flames died away, and then pursued their journey.

*   *   *   *   *

Years passed away. From the pile of ashes left by the departed oak sprang lovely flowers, which charmed the eyes of all the trees in the forest, and atoned, in a great measure, for the loss of their noble companion.

After a brief period workmen were seen in the forest felling the trees.

"Ah!" exclaimed the old pine who had refused to give its life for the travelers, "I don't see as we have gained anything. If our life is to go, it might as well have gone by the fire as by the axe."

"Just so," answered the beach, "only if we had perished by the fire we might now be coming again into another form of life, as our oak seems to be, from that pile of dust and ashes; for see what lovely blossoms are coming forth from that unsightly heap of dust."

"I heard the workmen say that all these trees were to be cleared away, and houses erected on the land," remarked a trembling ash, and her leaves quivered beyond their wont with the terror of this new thought.

"And that will surely be the end of us," moaned the pine.

"Our happy life is all over now," said a small fir, who would have continued bemoaning their destiny had not her attention at that instant been arrested by two forms entering the forest. They went to the spot where once stood the brave oak, and gazed admiringly on the lovely tinted blossoms. They had heard of the sacrifice of the tree, and had come to gaze upon its resurrection.

"We will gather some for our festival to-night," they said, and stooped to pluck the fragrant blossoms.

The fire had not destroyed the consciousness of the oak: its soul was still alive, enjoying its new form of existence, and it sent forth thrills of gratitude, which took the form of sweetest odor, filling the air around with fragrance. "Instead of losing my life it is being extended, even as the good leader of the people said," were its words as the two departed, bearing the flowers, instinct with its oak life, away.

Many went to the forest while the workmen were there, to gather the seeds of the rare blossoms to plant in their gardens.

How much of human life did the soul of the oak learn as it went forth thus amid the throngs of people; and how it rejoiced that it had given its life for the good of others, knowing not that greater bliss was in store for it! It was held in the hands of the aged; it crowned fair brows; it was carried to the bedside of the suffering; it was laid upon the caskets of the dead; it was planted by the door of the cottage and reared in the conservatories of the rich,--everywhere admired and welcomed. Was not this life indeed worth all the pain and heat of the flames, and the loss of its once statelier and loftier form?

It never sighed for its forest home, but often longed to know of the fate of its brother trees. One day a child, bearing in her hand one of its blossoms, wandered to the ground where once arose the tall trees. The eyes of the oak, through the flower, looked in vain for its kindred. None were standing. They had all been felled and their wood converted into dwellings,--a useful but less beautiful form of existence than that which the oak possessed,--and they learned, after a time, that it is only by apparent destruction that life can be reconstructed. But they could only have the experiences which came within the scope of their life; and the oak was more than ever satisfied with its own, and rejoiced that it had passed through the refining element, losing thereby only its grosser form. It filled the air with the fragrance of its gratitude. Whenever it wished to journey, the winds, who were its friends, conveyed its seeds to any portion of the earth it designated. Its blossoms were not only bright to the eye, and their odor sweet to the sense of smell, but the leaves of the plant were healing. Three forces connected it with human life: so that it was in constant action, and its highest joy lay in the consciousness of its increased usefulness.

XXIII.
STRANGERS.

In a large and elegant mansion dwelt a wealthy man who had three lovely daughters. The house was built on an eminence upon the banks of a river which wound like a thread of silver through the valleys for many miles. Afar from the mansion were a large number of cottages, in which dwelt carpenters, shipbuilders, gardeners, and some of every trade. Most of them were good and honest people, though tinged with the love of earthly gains, and many of them, too, often crushed many of the soul's finer and better emotions in the greedy love of material things. The owner of the mansion sorrowed over this failing of theirs, and, to rid them of it, devised a plan by which to give those who wished an opportunity to be led by their better nature, and forget, for the time, self and gain.

Accordingly, he told his daughters to deck themselves in their richest apparel and ornaments, which were rare and choice, and then to throw over the whole large and unsightly cloaks, so that the disguise might be perfect, and conceal all the splendor beneath. To each he gave a purse filled with gold to bestow upon the one who should welcome and give them shelter.

At evening he went forth with them to the narrow street, and bade them knock at the doors of the cottages, while he waited outside, and see who would admit and give food and shelter to travelers in need. They obeyed him, and first approached a dimly-lighted cottage. Making known their presence by a gentle rap, the door was opened by a woman of large and coarse features, whose eyes had no welcome in their rude stare. She scarcely waited for the words of the travelers to be spoken, ere she gruffly answered, "No: we have neither room nor food for beggars," and closed the door abruptly.

They applied next upon the opposite side, saying to the man who opened the door, "Can you feed and give shelter to three weary travelers?"

"We have no food to waste, and our home is scarcely large enough for ourselves," he replied, and quickly shut the door upon them.

The same answer came from all, and they turned to their parent, saying, "Shall we try any more?"

"There are but two more: try all; see if one at least can be found not wholly selfish; and, as you are not truly in need of their bounties, you can well afford to importune and be denied." He then guided his children to the end of the street.

"This one looks quite gay compared with the others," said the eldest of the daughters, as they all looked on the well-lit rooms, and beheld forms flitting to and fro within.

"We shall certainly be admitted here," said the others.

But the parent kept his council, and was invisible while they rapped at the door, which was opened by a bright and rather stylish-looking girl, who gazed wonderingly on the group.

"Can you give us shelter for a night, and a little food?" asked the eldest.

"Not we, indeed: we have just spent all our money for a merry-making for our brother Jack, who has just come home from sea. Not we: we have not one bit of room to spare; for all our friends are here."

"But we are weary, and ask rest and food," pleaded one of the three; and her eyes wandered to the well-filled tables.

"Yes: but what we have is for our company and ourselves--not for beggars," said the girl, and she closed the door upon them.

"Shall we try again, father?" they said to their parent.

"Just this one, which is the last," he answered, leading them to the door of a cot where dwelt a poor and lonely widow.

They paused at the threshold, for a voice was heard within, low and sweet; yet they heard the words of the kneeling form, in deep petition, saying, "Give me, O Father, my daily bread; forgive me my trespasses, and lead me not into temptation. For thine is the kingdom, and the power, and the glory, forever and forever. Amen."

She arose at that instant. A gentle knock was heard. Without delay she opened it, and smiled upon the strangers, who asked for more than she could give.

"I have shelter, but no food; yet enter and be welcome," she said, and opened wide the door.

They passed in, and left their parent, whom they knew would soon follow, outside.

"I grieve that I have no food to offer thee," said the woman, "but come to my fireside; for the evening air is chilly, and you must need rest."

She placed for them her only chairs beside the fire, saying, "I am glad you come to-night; for this is my last fuel, and to-morrow eve it will be all dark and chill within my dwelling."

The eldest bowed to the woman gracefully, and threw aside her cloak; and at once the others followed her example.

Great was the surprise of the widow. She thought her senses had departed, and, for an instant, had no voice, no words, naught but wonder beaming from her eyes, so sudden and great was the surprise. Another gentle rap at that instant seemed to help her to find herself, and she was hastening to open it, when the eldest one said, "It is our father, come to thank you for admitting angels in disguise; for, though not angels in form, we hope to prove such by our administration to your needs." And they laid upon her only table the purses of gold.

"He will ever give daily bread to those who forget not to entertain strangers," said their father to the widow, as they took their leave of one who had not refused to receive strangers.

The next morning there was great commotion in the neighborhood; for the widow had been seen to exchange gold for bread at one of the shops; but greater still was their surprise when she told them, as they flocked around her dwelling, that it was given by three strangers who had asked for bread and shelter the night before.

"Three strangers!" exclaimed they all. "They must be the same that called at our dwellings. What fools we were that we did not let them in!"

"Nay: it but shows how dead you were in sympathy for human need," spoke a voice among them, which, as they turned, they found to be that of the owner of the mansion.

Shame and confusion came over their faces; for he had long been their benefactor, both in words of counsel and deeds of kindness. Their eyes fell to the ground, as he in gentle tones chided them for their lack of kindness and want of faith in the Father's love. "He who giveth not in another's need shall receive none in his own," he continued; "and let the lesson taught you by the experience you have just had, and the example of the poor widow, last you through all the years of your life; for she refused not the strangers whom you turned from your doors the shelter which they apparently needed."

"But they were not cold and hungry," said one of the group.

"The demand upon your sympathies was just the same; for you knew not to the contrary," he answered, and they could not but feel the truth of his words.

The lesson was not lost; for in after years they grew less mercenary, more kindly of heart, and never again closed their doors to strangers asking aid.

The Codes Of Hammurabi And Moses
W. W. Davies

QTY

The discovery of the Hammurabi Code is one of the greatest achievements of archaeology, and is of paramount interest, not only to the student of the Bible, but also to all those interested in ancient history...

Religion   **ISBN:** *1-59462-338-4*   **Pages:**132
MSRP $12.95

The Theory of Moral Sentiments
Adam Smith

QTY

This work from 1749. contains original theories of conscience amd moral judgment and it is the foundation for systemof morals.

Philosophy **ISBN:** *1-59462-777-0*   **Pages:**536
MSRP $19.95

Jessica's First Prayer
Hesba Stretton

QTY

In a screened and secluded corner of one of the many railway-bridges which span the streets of London there could be seen a few years ago, from five o'clock every morning until half past eight, a tidily set-out coffee-stall, consisting of a trestle and board, upon which stood two large tin cans, with a small fire of charcoal burning under each so as to keep the coffee boiling during the early hours of the morning when the work-people were thronging into the city on their way to their daily toil...

Childrens   **ISBN:** *1-59462-373-2*
Pages:84
MSRP $9.95

My Life and Work
Henry Ford

QTY

Henry Ford revolutionized the world with his implementation of mass production for the Model T automobile. Gain valuable business insight into his life and work with his own auto-biography... "We have only started on our development of our country we have not as yet, with all our talk of wonderful progress, done more than scratch the surface. The progress has been wonderful enough but..."

Biographies/   **ISBN:** *1-59462-198-5*
Pages:300
MSRP $21.95

The Art of Cross-Examination
Francis Wellman

QTY

I presume it is the experience of every author, after his first book is published upon an important subject, to be almost overwhelmed with a wealth of ideas and illustrations which could readily have been included in his book, and which to his own mind, at least, seem to make a second edition inevitable. Such certainly was the case with me; and when the first edition had reached its sixth impression in five months, I rejoiced to learn that it seemed to my publishers that the book had met with a sufficiently favorable reception to justify a second and considerably enlarged edition. ..

Pages:412

Reference   ISBN: *1-59462-647-2*   *MSRP $19.95*

On the Duty of Civil Disobedience
Henry David Thoreau

QTY

Thoreau wrote his famous essay, On the Duty of Civil Disobedience, as a protest against an unjust but popular war and the immoral but popular institution of slave-owning. He did more than write—he declined to pay his taxes, and was hauled off to gaol in consequence. Who can say how much this refusal of his hastened the end of the war and of slavery ?

Law   ISBN: *1-59462-747-9*   **Pages:48**
MSRP $7.45

Dream Psychology Psychoanalysis for Beginners
Sigmund Freud

QTY

Sigmund Freud, born Sigismund Schlomo Freud (May 6, 1856 - September 23, 1939), was a Jewish-Austrian neurologist and psychiatrist who co-founded the psychoanalytic school of psychology. Freud is best known for his theories of the unconscious mind, especially involving the mechanism of repression; his redefinition of sexual desire as mobile and directed towards a wide variety of objects; and his therapeutic techniques, especially his understanding of transference in the therapeutic relationship and the presumed value of dreams as sources of insight into unconscious desires.

Pages:196

Psychology   ISBN: *1-59462-905-6*   *MSRP $15.45*

The Miracle of Right Thought
Orison Swett Marden

QTY

Believe with all of your heart that you will do what you were made to do. When the mind has once formed the habit of holding cheerful, happy, prosperous pictures, it will not be easy to form the opposite habit. It does not matter how improbable or how far away this realization may see, or how dark the prospects may be, if we visualize them as best we can, as vividly as possible, hold tenaciously to them and vigorously struggle to attain them, they will gradually become actualized, realized in the life. But a desire, a longing without endeavor, a yearning abandoned or held indifferently will vanish without realization.

Pages:360

Self Help   ISBN: *1-59462-644-8*   *MSRP $25.45*

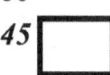

QTY

The Rosicrucian Cosmo-Conception Mystic Christianity *by Max Heindel* ISBN: *1-59462-188-8* **$38.95**
The Rosicrucian Cosmo-conception is not dogmatic, neither does it appeal to any other authority than the reason of the student. It is: not controversial, but is: sent forth in the, hope that it may help to clear... *New Age/Religion Pages 646*

Abandonment To Divine Providence *by Jean-Pierre de Caussade* ISBN: *1-59462-228-0* **$25.95**
"The Rev. Jean Pierre de Caussade was one of the most remarkable spiritual writers of the Society of Jesus in France in the 18th Century. His death took place at Toulouse in 1751. His works have gone through many editions and have been republished... *Inspirational/Religion Pages 400*

Mental Chemistry *by Charles Haanel* ISBN: *1-59462-192-6* **$23.95**
Mental Chemistry allows the change of material conditions by combining and appropriately utilizing the power of the mind. Much like applied chemistry creates something new and unique out of careful combinations of chemicals the mastery of mental chemistry... *New Age Pages 354*

The Letters of Robert Browning and Elizabeth Barret Barrett 1845-1846 vol II ISBN: *1-59462-193-4* **$35.95**
by Robert Browning and Elizabeth Barrett *Biographies Pages 596*

Gleanings In Genesis (volume I) *by Arthur W. Pink* ISBN: *1-59462-130-6* **$27.45**
Appropriately has Genesis been termed "the seed plot of the Bible" for in it we have, in germ form, almost all of the great doctrines which are afterwards fully developed in the books of Scripture which follow... *Religion/Inspirational Pages 420*

The Master Key *by L. W. de Laurence* ISBN: *1-59462-001-6* **$30.95**
In no branch of human knowledge has there been a more lively increase of the spirit of research during the past few years than in the study of Psychology, Concentration and Mental Discipline. The requests for authentic lessons in Thought Control, Mental Discipline and... *New Age/Business Pages 422*

The Lesser Key Of Solomon Goetia *by L. W. de Laurence* ISBN: *1-59462-092-X* **$9.95**
This translation of the first book of the "Lernegton" which is now for the first time made accessible to students of Talismanic Magic was done, after careful collation and edition, from numerous Ancient Manuscripts in Hebrew, Latin, and French... *New Age/Occult Pages 92*

Rubaiyat Of Omar Khayyam *by Edward Fitzgerald* ISBN:*1-59462-332-5* **$13.95**
Edward Fitzgerald, whom the world has already learned, in spite of his own efforts to remain within the shadow of anonymity, to look upon as one of the rarest poets of the century, was born at Bredfield, in Suffolk, on the 31st of March, 1809. He was the third son of John Purcell... *Music Pages 172*

Ancient Law *by Henry Maine* ISBN: *1-59462-128-4* **$29.95**
The chief object of the following pages is to indicate some of the earliest ideas of mankind, as they are reflected in Ancient Law, and to point out the relation of those ideas to modern thought. *Religion/History Pages 452*

Far-Away Stories *by William J. Locke* ISBN: *1-59462-129-2* **$19.45**
"Good wine needs no bush, but a collection of mixed vintages does. And this book is just such a collection. Some of the stories I do not want to remain buried for ever in the museum files of dead magazine-numbers an author's not unpardonable vanity..." *Fiction Pages 272*

Life of David Crockett *by David Crockett* ISBN: *1-59462-250-7* **$27.45**
"Colonel David Crockett was one of the most remarkable men of the times in which he lived. Born in humble life, but gifted with a strong will, an indomitable courage, and unremitting perseverance... *Biographies/New Age Pages 424*

Lip-Reading *by Edward Nitchie* ISBN: *1-59462-206-X* **$25.95**
Edward B. Nitchie, founder of the New York School for the Hard of Hearing, now the Nitchie School of Lip-Reading, Inc, wrote "LIP-READING Principles and Practice". The development and perfecting of this meritorious work on lip-reading was an undertaking... *How-to Pages 400*

A Handbook of Suggestive Therapeutics, Applied Hypnotism, Psychic Science ISBN: *1-59462-214-0* **$24.95**
by Henry Munro *Health/New Age/Health/Self-help Pages 376*

A Doll's House: and Two Other Plays *by Henrik Ibsen* ISBN: *1-59462-112-8* **$19.95**
Henrik Ibsen created this classic when in revolutionary 1848 Rome. Introducing some striking concepts in playwriting for the realist genre, this play has been studied the world over. *Fiction/Classics/Plays 308*

The Light of Asia *by sir Edwin Arnold* ISBN: *1-59462-204-3* **$13.95**
In this poetic masterpiece, Edwin Arnold describes the life and teachings of Buddha. The man who was to become known as Buddha to the world was born as Prince Gautama of India but he rejected the worldly riches and abandoned the reigns of power when... *Religion/History/Biographies Pages 170*

The Complete Works of Guy de Maupassant *by Guy de Maupassant* ISBN: *1-59462-157-8* **$16.95**
"For days and days, nights and nights, I had dreamed of that first kiss which was to consecrate our engagement, and I knew not on what spot I should put my lips..." *Fiction/Classics Pages 240*

The Art of Cross-Examination *by Francis L. Wellman* ISBN: *1-59462-309-0* **$26.95**
Written by a renowned trial lawyer, Wellman imparts his experience and uses case studies to explain how to use psychology to extract desired information through questioning. *How-to/Science/Reference Pages 408*

Answered or Unanswered? *by Louisa Vaughan* ISBN: *1-59462-248-5* **$10.95**
Miracles of Faith in China *Religion Pages 112*

The Edinburgh Lectures on Mental Science (1909) *by Thomas* ISBN: *1-59462-008-3* **$11.95**
This book contains the substance of a course of lectures recently given by the writer in the Queen Street Hall, Edinburgh. Its purpose is to indicate the Natural Principles governing the relation between Mental Action and Material Conditions... *New Age/Psychology Pages 148*

Ayesha *by H. Rider Haggard* ISBN: *1-59462-301-5* **$24.95**
Verily and indeed it is the unexpected that happens! Probably if there was one person upon the earth from whom the Editor of this, and of a certain previous history, did not expect to hear again... *Classics Pages 380*

Ayala's Angel *by Anthony Trollope* ISBN: *1-59462-352-X* **$29.95**
The two girls were both pretty, but Lucy who was twenty-one who supposed to be simple and comparatively unattractive, whereas Ayala was credited, as her Bombwhat romantic name might show, with poetic charm and a taste for romance. Ayala when her father died was nineteen... *Fiction Pages 484*

The American Commonwealth *by James Bryce* ISBN: *1-59462-286-8* **$34.45**
An interpretation of American democratic political theory. It examines political mechanics and society from the perspective of Scotsman James Bryce *Politics Pages 572*

Stories of the Pilgrims *by Margaret P. Pumphrey* ISBN: *1-59462-116-0* **$17.95**
This book explores pilgrims religious oppression in England as well as their escape to Holland and eventual crossing to America on the Mayflower, and their early days in New England... *History Pages 268*

QTY

The Fasting Cure *by Sinclair Upton* ISBN: *1-59462-222-1* **$13.95**
In the Cosmopolitan Magazine for May, 1910, and in the Contemporary Review (London) for April, 1910, I published an article dealing with my experiences in fasting. I have written a great many magazine articles, but never one which attracted so much attention... New Age/Self Help/Health Pages 164

Hebrew Astrology *by Sepharial* ISBN: *1-59462-308-2* **$13.45**
In these days of advanced thinking it is a matter of common observation that we have left many of the old landmarks behind and that we are now pressing forward to greater heights and to a wider horizon than that which represented the mind-content of our progenitors... Astrology Pages 144

Thought Vibration or The Law of Attraction in the Thought World ISBN: *1-59462-127-6* **$12.95**

by William Walker Atkinson *Psychology/Religion Pages 144*

Optimism *by Helen Keller* ISBN: *1-59462-108-X* **$15.95**
Helen Keller was blind, deaf, and mute since 19 months old, yet famously learned how to overcome these handicaps, communicate with the world, and spread her lectures promoting optimism. An inspiring read for everyone... Biographies/Inspirational Pages 84

Sara Crewe *by Frances Burnett* ISBN: *1-59462-360-0* **$9.45**
In the first place, Miss Minchin lived in London. Her home was a large, dull, tall one, in a large, dull square, where all the houses were alike, and all the sparrows were alike, and where all the door-knockers made the same heavy sound... Childrens/Classic Pages 88

The Autobiography of Benjamin Franklin *by Benjamin Franklin* ISBN: *1-59462-135-7* **$24.95**
The Autobiography of Benjamin Franklin has probably been more extensively read than any other American historical work, and no other book of its kind has had such ups and downs of fortune. Franklin lived for many years in England, where he was agent... Biographies/History Pages 332

Name	
Email	
Telephone	
Address	
City, State ZIP	

☐ **Credit Card**   ☐ **Check / Money Order**

Credit Card Number	
Expiration Date	
Signature	

Please Mail to: Book Jungle
PO Box 2226
Champaign, IL 61825
or Fax to: 630-214-0564

ORDERING INFORMATION
web*: www.bookjungle.com*
email*: sales@bookjungle.com*
fax*: 630-214-0564*
mail*: Book Jungle PO Box 2226 Champaign, IL 61825*
or PayPal *to sales@bookjungle.com*

Please contact us for bulk discounts

DIRECT-ORDER TERMS

**20% Discount if You Order
Two or More Books**
Free Domestic Shipping!
Accepted: Master Card, Visa,
Discover, American Express